Cassi Eubank

Diary of an

Ugly Sweater

Your diary always tells the true story

ISBN – 978-0-9961421-0-6

Diary of an Ugly Sweater

www.DiaryOfAnUglySweater.com
www.CassiEubank.com

To my mother, Pat Eubank. Thank you for teaching me the importance of being myself and always embracing those things which make me happy.

To my son, Leif Erik Johnsen. You are the source of such joy and happiness in my life and you have taught me more than I could ever teach you.

To my daughter, Elissa Johnsen. You are the best mother a woman could want for her grandchild, and a beautiful soul.

To my precious Elliot. You make me smile every time I think of you. Always dream big and always, always believe in yourself.

And to my husband and best friend, John. Thank you for supporting me in everything I do and never trying to change anything about me. I love everything about you, too.

Family isn't an important thing, it's everything.
~ Michael J. Fox

Foreword

One of the things in life I highly recommend is engaging in activities that make you happy and bring you pleasure. Writing this book was so much more fun than I thought it could be. Getting into the character of a sweater to write from her perspective was fascinating. The character development of her "framily" was also a great exercise.

Yet for all I got out of writing the book, it was designed to capture your imagination and empathy, and take you for a light ride with serious undertones. It was crafted to bring up situations, issues and opportunities that occur in everyday life, and provides real-life solutions.

No matter how different we are, our challenges are all so similar. I have always believed we are more alike than different, and it is those very differences that are to be celebrated. Through my experience and skills as a Results Coach, Neuro Linguistic practitioner and psychology trainer, I understand that storytelling is one of the best ways to send a message directly to the subconscious mind and make it stick. It is my intention that by laying out solutions and options in the story that allow the sweater to thrive in the face of adversity, your subconscious mind will then go to this new information when seeking the best solution for your own experiences and growth opportunities.

You won't need to look for the lessons. Some will be obvious, some will not. Just relax and enjoy the journey into the world of a sweater. The diary will tell all of her secrets.

PART I

It's the end of the world as she knows it …

I know as many of you read this, you will judge me. I have done some things I'm not proud of, even if my reasons seemed valid at the time. I am tattered and torn, and I realize no needle will ever make me right again.

Truth be told, I straight up lost it. The pressure was too much. I lost track of what was really important and got swept away in the madness. The emotions are still raw and I think it's best if you just read my diary. It will explain everything.

Sunday, December 1
Dear Diary,

Wow. What a day! Since this is my first entry in my new diary, I guess I should start by introducing myself. My name is Sophie, and I am a Christmas sweater.

Right now I am so excited, yet I'm sad at the same time. Tomorrow I will be leaving for Warehouse City. I have lived my whole life in the factory, all eight days of it, and I am pretty comfortable here.

I come from the "Tree with Pom Balls" family. I've heard us referred to as SKU 98772654. The tree on my front side is the kind that people decorate at Christmas and poms are little balls of yarn, that are made by tying lots of tiny pieces of yarn together. The yarn fans out into a ball shape and looks like the larger ball ornaments that are put on real trees during the holiday season. The poms are attached to the tree on the front of me so it looks like a decorated Christmas tree.

Everyone in my family looks exactly the same. Even our poms are the same color and in the same place on each of us. They have inspectors who make sure we are all alike. Some of us are smaller than others, but that is about the only discernable difference.

I happen to be a small size. So are my sisters Marci, Chloe, Jessica and Patricia. They are fantastic and I love them so much. At night, we shake our poms and sing "Jingle Bells" for

3

everyone. The whole factory loves it, and they all join in by the second verse. I love singing more than anything in the world, but I was terrified at first because I didn't think people would like the way I sang. Chloe gave me some good advice that really helped.

"Instead of telling yourself that you feel nervous, tell yourself you are feeling excited because you have the chance to do something you love," she explained. "Make it a happy feeling instead of a scary feeling!"

Then she said if I wanted to sing, she would sing with me so I wouldn't be alone.

With Chloe by my side, I had the courage to sing in front of all the sweaters, and now I really get excited every time I have the chance to harmonize with the others. I get better each time I sing, and even Kevin from the "Santa Sitting on the Toilet" family of sweaters said I was really good.

My sisters and brothers tell me I shouldn't be talking to anyone from that sweater family, because they think there is something "off" about them. Still, I thought it was very nice of Kev to say that. It really made me feel good, and he and I are friends, anyway.

I told Jessica that who I could or couldn't talk to was my decision. She was only mad at me for half a day, but it felt like forever. Ever since she started making eyes at the boy in the "Hanging Jingle Balls" sweater family, she stopped being so judgmental. I can't say out loud what the sweaters in that family look like because they are a little vulgar, and let's just leave it at that!

Tonya, Leila and Annie are the little ones. They are size Extra

Small. Even though we all look alike, there is something so cute about them. Leila has this giggle that is so adorable it makes you laugh when you hear it. She thinks she is a comedian because when she tells a joke, she always laughs afterwards. Everyone roars with laughter at the sound of her giggle, and she believes it's because she is funny. She's really not funny at all, but it is hysterical the way she laughs so hard at herself and thinks she's the funniest sweater ever knitted.

Richard, Larry, Timothy, Irina and Elissa are my Medium-sized brothers and sisters. They are all so sensible and, truth be told, are the real comedians in the Sweater Factory. When the workers leave the factory at 6:00 pm sharp every night, they repeat some of the comedies that the janitor puts on the television when he cleans up at night. Old Eddie's favorite channel is the Comedy Network, so we see lots of comedians and funny shows. There is one called *The Big Bang Theory*, and the Mediums act out some of the scenes for us when we are alone before Old Eddie comes.

Jason says that Sheldon is the best character on that show. Since he is the only X-Large in our family, nobody disputes his opinion. Tom from the "Flamingo and Ostrich Feather" sweater family disagrees. He likes Penny and does a pretty lame impression of her that is hilarious.

All my large brothers and sisters are so very different. I know this might seem weird since we all are made from the same yarn, but it's true. Mark and Kurt are the quiet ones. Rarely do they talk and when they do, it's something dark and snarky. They finish each other's sentences in a way that's cool and creepy all at the same time. They are a little misunderstood, and I think they secretly like being that way, because people are hesitant to approach them. I hope this doesn't hurt their chances of finding a home. They are both very attractive, if I do say so myself (wink, wink).

Terry, Helen and Naomi are my large sisters. They are so creative and make up stories of the homes we will find once we get to our stores where we can be chosen by people shopping there.

Ah yes, there it is again; the thought of leaving the only place I've ever known and going to my next destination. I will miss the men and women who made us. Kelly is like a mom to me. She is the one who made me with her own gentle, tender hands. She gave me this diary to write in and record my great adventures as I leave the factory and head out to the great and wonderful world beyond. I think I will miss her the most. I am not sure if they will have television at Warehouse City. I may never see *The Big Bang Theory* again. And what will happen when I do get to the warehouse? There are so many questions. For now, I am tired. I think it is time for bed. I promise to write to you tomorrow.

Monday, December 2
Dear Diary,

I'd heard all the rumors about what it was like at Warehouse City. The sweater makers spoke about how we would be shipped off to a huge warehouse more than 100 times larger than the factory where we were created. They talked about what the other sweater families looked like, but nothing they said could have prepared me for the day I had today.

There are transportation specialists that get us ready for our big trip. The man who was telling the others what to do goes by the name of Henry. I know this because I saw it on the name tag on this uniform shirt; also, the others that work in his group called him Boss.

It's funny how the workers at the factory don't look like their families. There are four people in the transportation specialist's family. Henry has light hair, sort of a sandy blonde. Another one has hair as orange as the round orange thing I've seen him eat. The two others have very black hair; one very short and the other very long. It's kind of confusing. I like the way us sweaters do it better. It is so much easier to know who belongs with which family!

The workers got to the factory at 7:00 am sharp. As soon as the transportation specialists arrived at the factory, they went into the main office and came back with several sheets of paper. After much discussion among the four, they started pulling cardboard sheets from the rack on the wall. Once they were all pulled, two of the workers started to push the cardboard sheets in different directions, creating a box shape. Then they would slide it over to the second guy and say, "Tape it up." The second guy then put a clear strip of sticky stuff along the box to hold the flaps together.

A few of the women factory workers went over to the "Hanging Jingle Balls" sweater family. Each sweater was lifted up, one at a time. When the woman was satisfied with the looks of the sweater, they would put a sticker on it with "Inspected By" and a number after it. Each worker had a different number. Could that be their name, just a number? The thought of that seems kind of sad to me; to only have a number as a name. I love my name, Sophie. I even wrote a song about my name. Maybe I'll sing it for you later.

After the worker put her number on each sweater, she carefully placed a protective plastic coat over it, giving the sweater an extra shine. I looked forward to being wrapped in my own travel coat.

Finally, all the Hanging Balls were given to the transportation specialists, or "TSs", as we called them for short. They separated the family out by sizes and placed a blanket of plastic around each of them. It was like we were getting our own bedroom as we snuggled up for the ride to Warehouse City.

I was a little nervous about leaving the place where I was created. Wait, scratch that; I was EXCITED! See how I did that; how I changed the way I phrased my feelings so they work for me? Chloe taught me that cool trick yesterday.

After being at the factory over a week and getting to know the people who worked there, I had become pretty comfortable.

8

There were only five other sweater families at our factory, but I've been told there are almost 100 more at the warehouse. I wondered if the other sweaters will like me ... if I would fit in. I am not quite sure why I worry about such silly things, but a part of me admittedly does feel that way.

But while I had those emotions, I also couldn't wait to see all these new-to-me sweaters ... would they be glamorous and handsome or funny? Would they be silly and smart? No matter what, I knew I would love them all, which is why I wasn't sure why I worried so much about them liking me.

I do know that I am kind, fun and caring, so of course they will like me, too. It's just that I heard one of my brothers saying things that weren't nice about someone in the "Santa Sitting on the Toilet" family. I know I'm not perfect, either, so I hope all the other sweaters will overlook my faults and just see my good heart and like me, anyway.

Those thoughts vanished when we were taken to be prepared for travel. It was finally our family's turn. I was glad to see Kelly, my creator, as she picked me up to inspect me. I could see the love in her eyes and I knew I would miss her, even though my destiny was elsewhere – with someone who would love and take care of me forever. *My forever person.*

She fondly brushed me off and brought me close to her chest for a final goodbye, then pulled me away and proudly placed her sticker on me. My creator's name is 13. All this time spent near her, and I never knew. I thought it was "Kelly" because the tag on the shirt she wears every day says that. I like that number so I guess I like the name, but it's still a little weird.

Once our family was snugly boxed up for the ride, we felt the motion of the box as we were moved out of the factory building.

I heard someone call out to put us in Truck 73. I guess the trucks have numbers for names, too. Maybe we sweaters are more evolved and that's why we get to have real names? Or maybe numbers are more evolved? (I know what you're thinking, and you're right. I have the "oh look ... a shiny red ball" syndrome. My creator, Kelly, or "Number 13" has it, too. That's how I learned about it. It means that I get easily distracted.)

When all the boxes of sweaters were in Truck 73, we heard its rear doors close. There was a muffled conversation coming from outside the truck, followed by a short silence before the engine started up. There was this really cool shimmying motion I've never felt before when the engine roared to life. Then Truck 73 was moving, and we all started talking at once. I wasn't the only one nervous and excited about what was to come.

After about an hour, my sisters and I started singing for everyone. Have I mentioned how much I love singing? I love everything about it. I love how it bonds people. I love hearing multiple sweaters harmonize, and I love how I feel when I am singing. When you find something that makes you this happy, you know you are meant to do it as often as possible. I know I was meant to sing!

I'm not sure when we all finally fell asleep, but all the sweaters from all the families were deep in slumber when the rear doors of the truck were thrown open and people started taking the boxes out of Truck 73. I thought that perhaps we might get to meet everyone today, but they kept us in the boxes. That's fine with me because I want to be at my best when I do meet the others.

Tuesday, December 3
Dear Diary,

When I woke up, we were still in the same box as when we'd
left the factory. There was so much noise in the warehouse. My
curiosity was tugging at me; it was so strong it was almost an
ache. I couldn't wait for them to open the boxes and let us out. I
wanted to finally see all the other sweater families the factory
workers at home talked about so much. Would they be pretty?
Would they be funny? Would they be nice? The questions raced
through my mind.

It seemed like forever, but before the middle of the day break
where all the workers leave the big room we were in, they
finally got to our box. I heard the workers refer to the break as
"lunchtime." Anyway, after being boxed up for over 24 hours,
the lights seemed very bright at first, and it took a few moments
to adjust to it. Once my vision cleared, I saw that we were in the
corner, and was pleased to see that I had a clear view of the rest
of the warehouse. I could see everything except the office area
and the room behind the door they all went through at this so-
called lunchtime.

Even as I write this, several hours later, I still can't believe all
the different sweater families here! There must have been over
50 different families that I could see. There were sweaters with
ornaments and garland. One family had bells on them that
jingled, and another sweater family all lit up with the flip of a

switch. One of the workers slid the switch into the "on" position and called out for everyone to check out the flashing lights. Everyone looked over, smiling their approval. It was funny to see a couple of the sweaters on the far wall getting jealous of the attention the "All Lit Up" family was getting.

There were the Skinny Santas, the Gingerbread Ballerinas, the Sleighing Snowman, the Sexy Snowgirls, the Flaky Snowflakes and so many more. The jewels, the glitz, the glam, I love it all! They are all so beautiful. *I love this place!*

The worker who opened our box removed the plastic that bundled our family together. When she hung us up, we had just the one plastic coat that kept us nice and shiny. I liked it. It made me feel like I was dressed up and ready for a party. Being out of the box felt good, and it finally gave me a chance to really look around.

I guess I should tell you about my run-in with Stephanie, one of the Smalls from the "Sexy Snowgirls" family. I was looking over all the sweaters in the warehouse, taking it all in and basically just minding my own business.

The whole warehouse had begun to smell really good. Soon, the warehouse people started shifting in their seats a lot and looking over at this round thing on the wall. It has two lines on it, one large and one short, that move around the center of the circle. I think I heard someone call it a clock. When both black lines on the clock were pointing straight up, everyone stood up and headed for the doorway from which those incredible smells originated.

Their departure gave me a clear view of the Sexy Snowgirls. They were so incredibly beautiful. They were light blue and had snowflakes in the background that were shiny and silver, catching your attention every time the light reflected off them. The Sexy Snowgirls were created with three white poms, very similar to the ones on my tree, only they were much, much bigger. Stephanie's poms made up her head and her body. The top pom was small and acted as her head. The snowgirl had on bright lipstick made of ruby red glitter. Her eyes were cobalt blue with lashes that were almost three inches long. I heard the family joking with each other about having the best falsies. They batted their eyelashes as they were laughing, so I think "falsies" is a special name for extra-long eyelashes. Whatever you call them, their eyelashes were stunning!

The second pom was larger than the first and rested just below the top pom – and the bottom pom was bigger still. The family sports a row of red fringe around the top of the bottom pom. They say it's a skirt, but it is very short for a skirt! *Only two inches at best!* I heard several other families whispering about them, gossiping with judgemental looks on their faces. I don't care what they think; to me, the Sexy Snowgirls are an exotic clan.

But what really had the whole warehouse sweater community buzzing were the huge poms that were placed on top of their middle poms. These girls were definitely curvy, and all they had on was a very small bathing suit top! I heard words like "shocking" and "outrageous" used. One of the Extra Larges from the Gingerbread House gang even said that family was giving the whole sweater community a bad name.

Yet here I was, still drawn to them. I was looking at Stephanie, admiring her, wanting to take in every detail of her beauty.

"Hey tree face, what are you looking at?" she suddenly barked at me.

I was too shocked to speak. I wanted my first encounter with other sweaters to be a good one, but right now, this girl was calling me names and clearly had an attitude going on. I wasn't sure why she was calling me "tree face" or what I had done to upset her.

"Are you too stupid to talk, tree face?" she taunted.

Even though my whole family was next to me, I felt so alone. I had a challenge to rise up to, and I had to figure out what to do … and fast! All the sweaters in the warehouse were looking at us, watching to see what was going to go down.

"What's your favorite song?" I asked.

"Huh?" replied Steph.

"Your favorite song. What song do you love to sing?"

She was busy trying to come up with an answer to the question and forgot she was mad at me for a minute. I was beginning to think this might work.

"*Rudolph the Red-Nosed Reindeer*. Why, what's it to you?"

"Can you sing it without laughing?"

"Duh," she said, softening up as her curiosity took over.

"My family and I will teach you the funny version," I explained. "You sing it, and we will sing a back-up part. If you can go through the whole song without laughing, I will call you "Master" until we are shipped out of the warehouse. If you laugh, you just have to be nice to me. That's all. Do we have a deal?"

"You mean deal ... Master," she said and jumped right in to the Rudolph song.

Stephanie: Rudolph the red-nosed reindeer
Pom Trees: Reindeer
Stephanie: Had a very shiny nose
Pom Trees: Shiny Nose
Stephanie: And if you ever saw it
Pom Trees: Saw it
Stephanie: You would even say it glows
Pom Trees: Like a light bulb

I could see she was starting to smile, and I thought I actually heard a little snicker. While she loved being the center of attention, I realized that she was probably already mad before she ever encountered me. After all, others were saying bad things about her family ... and I was staring a little bit, too, though not because I agree with all the others. I was just fascinated.

Stephanie: All of the other reindeer
Pom Trees: Reindeer
Stephanie: Used to laugh and call him names
Pom Trees: Funny names, like Thaddeus Kokwazinski

That's when Stephanie completely lost it. I started laughing with her and soon all the sweaters were cackling and howling.

The warehouse workers were all starting to come back just as the laughter was subsiding, and we all went silent. I gathered all my nerve and whispered in Stephanie's direction before the workers were in earshot, "I was only looking at you because I think you are beautiful."

Steph stared at me for a full 10 seconds. The warehouse was

almost full, but she gave me a smile and a wink. It was an exaggerated move, and with her three-inch eyelashes it was all I could do to stifle the laugh that the workers were surely close enough now to hear. I was just glad she wasn't upset anymore and we could be friends, maybe even best friends – at least, until I found my forever home.

The warehouse people spent several hours after lunchtime cleaning up the warehouse. They swept and picked up all the paper on the floor. They were talking about special guests coming to visit tomorrow. I heard these people would pick six sweater families to be in a photo shoot for advertising, whatever that is. Out of those six families, they would take three of us, a Small, a Medium and a Large. I wasn't sure what all of that was about, but I was sure I'd find out tomorrow.

Once the warehouse people left for the day, we all got to know each other better. We sang songs, told jokes, and most fell asleep very early. Was it just yesterday that I was home and safe in my factory? Yet here I was today, among thousands of sweaters from over 100 different families.

There are only about a dozen of us still awake now, and I can barely stay awake as I finish today's entry.

Sleep tight, diary. I know I will.

Wednesday, December 4
Dear Diary,

The lights went on at a brisk 5:50 am this morning. I was not
used to getting up so early, and I could tell by the expressions on
the other sweaters that they were not too pleased, either. The
warehouse people went to the same workstations as yesterday.
They took turns going through the same doorway where the
good smells came from at yesterday's lunchtime, and came back
with cylinder-shaped mugs with handles; and each mug had
steam wafting from the top.

Today, everyone seemed more rushed, and the energy in the
warehouse was completely different. The workers continued
putting their ceramic mugs to their faces and tilting them back, a
little more each time. Once they tilted it at their face at a 100-
degree angle, they went back through the same doorway and
returned without the mug. Curious people, these warehouse
workers! I never noticed any of the workers do this back at the
factory. Seems the way people look and dress aren't their only
differences; apparently they have different habits and rules too.

Speaking of differences, our special guests arrived, and the
clothes they wore were very different from those of the workers.
There were three men and two women. All the women wore
shoes with a two- or three-inch pole coming out of the heels.
The way they walked was strange, as if they were trying to
balance on the shoe's stick; and honestly, their rear ends stuck
out a little. All the guests had jackets on that looked tailored, and

the men had long, thin pieces of cloth that were tied around their necks that hung down the front of their shirts. Each man had a different colored thin piece of cloth, although their suits looked like they came from the same family.

It was easy to see who was in charge; a man they called Sven. He was an authoritative blonde-haired man with spiked hair who walked back and forth, barking orders nonstop. Sven stopped in front of each rack of sweater families, tilting his head to the right and to the left, making little noises that weren't discernible. Finally he would shout, "nope," "maybe" or "definitely."

Sven's minions scurried behind him, voicing their agreement with his every choice and moving the racks of sweaters into the groups he chose for each rack. This wasn't feeling right to me. Who were they to judge us sweaters? Did they really think *they* were perfect? Seriously!

Of course, my whole attitude immediately changed when they picked our sweater family to be wheeled over to the "definitely" group. How exciting; we were chosen! I wasn't exactly sure what it was that made them decide to pick us, but it really felt good.

There were eight families chosen by the man with the purple strip of fabric around his neck. In addition to us, the Sexy Snowgirls made it, and I was glad after seeing how they were treated by the other sweaters yesterday. Also making it were the Santa Stuck in the Chimneys, the Tinsel Trees, the Gingerbread Ballerinas, the Sleighing Snowman, the Rudolphs with the light-up Noses, and the Kittens Opening Presents. A small part of me felt bad for those not chosen, but the excitement of being selected held my attention and was the stronger emotion.

Next, Sven and crew went through all eight racks and carefully examined each of us. One of the ladies was told to select a Small, Medium and a Large from our family. She came to our rack and pulled Marci, Chloe, Jessie, Pat and me from the rack first, placing us on the counter. Starting with Marci, she carefully examined every thread. She began picking at things and holding her up to the light, and I could tell my sister didn't like it. The lady found a loose thread and pulled it, causing Marci to flinch. The woman didn't even notice the pain she was inflicting, and just looked at the damage she caused by pulling the yarn.

"This one has a slight flaw," she exclaimed as she threw Marci to the side. I was so upset, I wanted to smack this woman for her treatment of my sister, but she snatched me up before I knew what happened, catching me off guard.

I didn't like how she went out of her way to look for all the negative things about me. Why couldn't she just look at how pretty I was? I didn't understand this and I didn't think I ever would. Why were they always looking for what is wrong instead of appreciating what is right?

After what seemed like forever, the woman cheerfully looked at me and informed me, "You will do." She then gave me to the man with a red piece of fabric tied around his neck, whose name was Ivan.

Ivan put all of the "final selections" on a rack and wheeled us to the back of the warehouse. My mind was racing. For some reason, I noticed that those same good smells were starting to come from the doorway again. Then I realized I didn't get a chance to say goodbye to anyone, and I was feeling a little scared. All I knew was we had to be "on set" for a "shoot" tomorrow.

I hoped Ivan was kidding when he motioned towards the rack where he placed the final selections and told one of the women, "These are the sweaters we will shoot tomorrow, Celeste. Make sure you cover them up so they stay nice and clean."

IT WAS US THEY PLANNED TO SHOOT? I saw what happened on television back at the factory when someone got shot. I thought they were just going to take pictures of us. It was a little scary not knowing what tomorrow would bring.

Ivan called out to the woman who brutalized my sister, "Get the door, Gwen!"

Gwen obliged, and as the door swung fully open, a bright light assaulted the darkness. Before we were wheeled outside, Celeste placed a large black piece of plastic over us so we couldn't see. I wondered if our destination was so secret that they wanted to blindfold us. Shooting us, blindfolds, what was going on I wondered.

I realized I just have an overactive imagination when I heard Sven tell Celeste and Gwen to make sure the protective cover was secure.

We were jostled around for a time, and then we were finally lifted. Soon, I felt the same vibrations I did when they moved us from the factory to the warehouse in the truck. The motion quickly lulled me to sleep.

Thursday, December 5
Dear Diary,

What a day! What a wonderful, magical day! Today was by far the best day of my life!

All the sweaters from the eight different families were comfortably hanging from a rack and were starting to wake up just as the lights went on in our new place. We couldn't see anything because the black plastic was still covering us, but the lights shone up from the bottom of the rack where it was uncovered.

At first, there were only the sounds of people moving things around and some muffled conversation. After a little while, however, there were lots of voices. Everyone sounded cheerful and they exchanged jokes despite the frantic pace that was obvious, even though we still couldn't see anything.

There was one voice that started shouting commands.

"Move the tree to the right."

"The star isn't straight. For heaven's sake, would someone please straighten out that star?"

"When will the models be ready?"

And I would be remiss to leave out the one thing he kept

repeating every five minutes, "Time is money people, TIME … IS … MONEY!"

The way he talked was different from anyone I'd ever heard. Every time he said a word with an "s" in it, he exaggerated it. It made me curious about him. Maybe he came from an exotic far away land?

It wasn't long before we all got to see what was happening around us. A tall woman with long yellow hair came and removed the black plastic from our rack. Instantly, we were all speechless.

The first thing that caught my eye was the tree. Right in front of me … a giant, majestic Christmas tree. I have a Christmas tree on me, but this one was unbelievable. It reached almost to the ceiling, and it was twice as big as the tall woman who'd taken the black plastic off us. It was the most beautiful thing I had ever seen.

The lights on the tree were all blue, flashing and winking. I surprised myself, as I was actually able to hold back a squeal of approval. Let me tell you, this was not an easy thing to do!

This tree had thousands of silver and blue balls all over it. They were shiny, completely unlike the yarn pom balls on my tree. There were other ornaments all over the tree, too. There were hundreds of lace angels, crystal icicles, and cinnamon sticks with silver and blue ribbons tied oh-so beautifully on each bundle. From the top, wide silver and blue ribbons cascaded down the side, each ribbon spiraling in one long, fantastic curl.

But what had me most awestruck was what I saw on the very top of the tree. It was truly mesmerizing. There was something so pure, so innocent, something that inspired hope and gratitude about the angel on top of the tall pine. Her skin was translucent and glowing, with a slight pink flush in her rosy cheeks. Her soft, childlike features made you love her and want to protect her all at the same time. Her silent light shone with the hope of eternal bliss and joy.

For several minutes, I stared in wonder at this heavenly winged tree topper, until Sven started shouting directions again. Just like that, the spell was broken.

To the right of the tree was a small brown house. It was covered with snow on its roof and was adorned with an abundance of candy, including its yard, which was fenced in by very large candy canes. I think it belonged to the Gingerbread family.

The Gingerbread family was much larger in stature than the Gingerbread Ballerinas on the sweater, and they dressed very different. They were wearing fancy clothes. The father wore a top hat and long jacket with a bow tie, while the mother wore a dress with stockings, a floppy hat and accessorized everything with an expensive-looking purse. They had a little gingerbread girl who was dressed just like her mom; and a gingerbread boy dressed just like his dad.

I find the differences in the way people dress, act and talk very intriguing. I have learned so much about people, sweaters and other living beings – especially considering I'm not yet even two weeks old! Still, I realize I have much I don't know … and I love studying and analyzing how people behave. I find our differences fascinating!

Looking around, I observed a wall that had a pile of bricks about three feet wide and four feet tall in front of it. There was a middle section with no bricks, just logs and a fire. On the floor in front of the fire sat a rug made out of some kind of big brown furry animal. Nearby, there were a couple of red chairs with high backs; and in between the chairs sat a small table upon which a plate of cookies and a glass of milk rested.

I was still taking it all in when Ivan shouted, "Wardrobe, get the sweaters on the models!"

Everything after that was a blur of activity. A small, baby-faced boy I had not seen before grabbed our rack, pushing us past a series of large panels separating the area decorated with the Christmas tree and Gingerbread House, before stopping in another area that was pure madness.

In this area there were boys, girls, men, and women sitting in chairs while other people were brushing colors on their faces. It was strange to see how people changed their faces by adding colors. I wondered what it would be like to paint and decorate myself. It all seemed so glamorous. I even saw some other people combing and spraying stuff into the hair of the seemingly important individuals who sat in the chairs.

After a few minutes we heard Sven's boss shouting, "Time is money people, TIME … IS … MONEY! Where are my models?"

The people in the chairs all jumped up, and at the same time several other people rushed over to our rack. They started grabbing and pulling at us, sliding us off our hangers. Each of us was given to a different person. I was assigned to one of the two young girls there to model. She didn't smile much, and I couldn't tell whether or not she liked me. This made me feel a little uncomfortable.

I always thought that when paired with my person, it would be different. I imagined that they would look at a bunch of sweaters and if they really liked me, they would try me on. If I liked them back, I would mold to them, we would be a fit, and they would take me home. That's always how I thought it would be, but things were not going according to the plan.

The girl with the sour face was rough with me. She didn't smile at all and kept picking at me, plucking imaginary pills off me. I didn't have any nubs or loose pieces of yarn. *Who did she think she was, anyway?*

She was still pulling at me when she, along with three other models, was called to the Christmas room. That's what I call that room, anyway. A small boy wearing a Rudolph sweater came with us. One of the assistants stopped the boy, turned up the hem of his sweater, and flipped the switch that made Rudolph's nose glow. Once the reindeer was shining, the man flipped the hem of the sweater back over and smoothed out the sweater so it looked good. I love it when Rudolph lights up!

There was another woman wearing Molly, one of the Medium Gingerbread Ballerinas, and a man who wore a sweater from the Sleighing Snowman family whose name I don't remember. (You should know that although the Sleighing Snowman family was a group of sweater vests, I still think of them as genuine sweaters, too. Not all the other sweaters felt that way, though.)

The man chosen to wear the sweater vest was wearing a strip of fabric tied to his neck, with a picture of Santa on it.

Sven starting telling the four models where to go, how to stand, and where to put their hands, clearly trying to impress the man with the accent. Meanwhile, a man controlling a small black box with a round cylinder protruding from the front kept bringing the box up to his eye and pressing a button. Each time he pressed it, a bright flash lit up. Over and over the light flashed, as the man kept making demands of the models. This is how they take pictures.

The models were very patient. I don't think I would be so nice if someone kept telling me what to do and how to act. I guess I'm just not fond of bossy people.

After a half hour of being blinded by the flashing box, also called a camera, and getting a mild headache from the man barking orders, the four models rushed back to the other side of the panels, pulled us off and threw us on the floor. Each model had a person handing them a new sweater. As the models put on the new sweaters, their assistants picked the old sweaters off the floor – me included – and put us back on a hanger before returning us to the rack.

As soon as the people left, Christin, one of the sweaters who was not selected to be photographed, started in with the questions.

"What happened?" "What was it like?" "Tell us everything!"

Two sweaters from each family had been brought in for the "shoot", but only one from each family was used. The eight sweaters that had been on the rack all day were now demanding to know what happened when we were taken out to the Christmas area, and what it was like.

I tried to answer, but I was exhausted. To be perfectly honest with you, I really wasn't completely sure what had taken place. Apparently, the three other sweaters felt the same way, as we gave vague answers and just wanted to be left alone to go to sleep.

Through various conversations we heard throughout the day, we surmised that we were the "featured" sweaters in what is called a "photo shoot." (I was relieved when I realized they "shoot" pictures, not the sweaters.) I also discovered our pictures were going to be in the newspaper. I shared what I knew and tried to explain that it wasn't "all that" like everyone thought. I told them they were lucky they got to stay and rest rather than being picked and pulled at, being pushed around, and getting tossed on the floor.

When the other four sweaters were returned to the rack, they covered us with the black plastic again. The darkness was a sweet relief as I, too, faded to the gentle black retreat of slumber. The eight sweaters who were not featured in the photographs began questioning the four newcomers, but even their excited chatter couldn't keep me awake.

Friday, December 6
Dear Diary,

I was jarred out of my blissful slumber by a sudden jolt. I tried
to gather my thoughts, but the darkness hampered much of my
progress. So much happened in such a short amount of time
yesterday, and I found myself initially wondering exactly where
I was as the fog of drowsiness lifted. I heard other sweaters
starting to yawn and show signs of waking as well, and after a
moment it all came back to me.

I heard a creaking noise, and then felt the cold air and saw the
light filtering up from the bottom of the rack holding the 16
Warehouse City sweaters that were set apart for the photo shoot.
Some of us might even be featured in newspapers! While it
wasn't all fun and games, I was glad I had the chance to
experience the whole modeling thing yesterday. But now, it
seemed we were back at Warehouse City, our current home for
the time being.

Once the rack was pushed into the warehouse, a worker came
over and removed the plastic from us. Once again, we could see.
I looked around, searching for my family. I quickly located them
right where they were when we left, on the shelf by the sink.

Four workers came to our rack, each taking the two sweaters
from the same family and bringing us to their benches. I
remembered the same woman who handled me when I got here
from the factory; that seemed like a lifetime ago now. Had it

been less than a week?

The woman looked me over with the same intense scowl she had on her face when I first arrived, looking to find any fault she could. She held me up to the light, lifted my sleeves, and even turned me inside out to give me a thorough once-over. It was a little uncomfortable and embarrassing, so I am not sure why it made me so happy when she broke out in a big smile of approval. I knew I didn't need her approval as long as I approved of myself, but it still felt good.

After a few minutes I decided to stop dwelling on this, because trying to figure it out was just a waste of time.

Next, she carefully placed tissue underneath me, neatly folded me, and put me on the shelf with my family. I could feel the love and peace that filled my heart just being with them. I couldn't wait for the good smells to come from the lunchroom, so all the workers would leave and I could talk to my family again.

When I am with family, I feel at home. And I must say, it feels good to be home!

Soon it was lunchtime again, and the moment the last worker left the room, the sweater community was buzzing. "What happened?" "What did you do?" "What was it like?"

It was kind of fun being the center of attention. I told everyone all about what was called "the set." I did my best to explain the beauty and brilliance of the tree. Molly was enamored with the Gingerbread House and went on about it for over five minutes. Those who did not go asked about being photographed and what it was like to be famous. I told them it was fun but not easy, and that I didn't feel famous at all.

Soon, all the sweater families started shouting questions, wanting to hear all about our adventures. We joyfully complied, having fun as we each told a slightly different version of how the events unfolded. I found it very interesting that we all did the exact same thing (other than the fact that only half of us got our pictures taken), yet we all had stories that varied. I noticed that the sweaters who typically had a positive outlook and tend to be happy had a much better experience than those who got grumpy and looked at the downside of things. I realized in that moment you can have a much better life simply by having a much better attitude about things.

The workers came back when lunchtime was over, and the sweaters again grew quiet. At night, however, when they left, the whole warehouse broke out in song. The warehouse workers had been playing music all day, and it seemed like the same 12 songs played over and over again so we learned the words. We all had a great time, and as I drifted off to sleep I couldn't help but imagine what wonderful surprises tomorrow would have in store for me.

Saturday, December 7
Dear Diary,

It seems times are changing fast. I can't help but wonder about my future. I overheard the other sweaters talking about what kind of person they want to own them. Marci wants someone who is hot all the time, so she can rest peacefully in the closet doing her meditation. Jessica said she wants to see a little action, so she's hoping for a woman who likes to party and will wear her all season long. Michael said he would be happy as long as his owner didn't sing Christmas carols all day. He was tired of them already, and he'd heard one of the workers complaining that some people play these songs for over a month after Christmas ends. Michael had gotten used to country music when we were at the factory, and the only Christmas carol he likes is the one about Grandma getting run over by a reindeer.

I wasn't sure what I wanted my person to be like, but I was getting a clear picture of what I did NOT want. I did not want someone who was always looking me over to make sure I am perfect.

Sure, I want to look my best. If I have a little wrinkle, go ahead and gently smooth me out until it's gone. But there's no reason to tug me so hard that I'm seeing stars! If I have a little fuzz, gently remove it; don't pull on my yarn and rip it out with the fuzz!

It made me wonder about humans. *Is that how they treat each other? Always trying to pull and manipulate them into what they want the other person to be, rather than helping them be their own personal best with gentle encouragement?*

Yet it seemed that the more I thought about what I did *not* want, the more I was assaulted by pinchy, picky, pully workers. For example, there were three young girls who worked in the far corner. When they learned I was in a photo shoot, they thought it would be fun it try me on and take pictures. They waited until the worker who looked over our family was "on break" … whatever that was. All I know is she left for the lunch area that always smells so good, so she wasn't there to protect me.

The three girls took turns putting me on. One would wear me while the other two held up these small boxes they sometimes talk into … or rapidly touch with their thumbs. They're called cell phones. I heard faint swishing noises as the girls touched the screens of the phone. Once the first girl was done, the next one tried me on. They didn't even seem to like me; they just wanted to get a picture of themselves wearing me.

I wondered if this was what it meant to be famous, and I decided that I didn't like being famous if this is what fame brought with it.

Once they all had their pictures, they placed me back on the shelf. They didn't take care to properly fold me, so my seams were getting a little sore. I also heard the girls call me an "ugly sweater" when they were trying me on, and they were laughing at me while they were taking pictures.

Everyone in Warehouse City witnessed this. The truth is, I was humiliated. I could pretend it didn't bother me, but I had turned bright red in my embarrassment, and just wanted to curl up into a ball and disappear.

When my protector finally returned, I was overjoyed. I heard someone call her Nikita. Oh precious Nikita … she became my angel.

She noticed at once that I was not comfortable, so she took me from the shelf and demanded to know who had mishandled me. The girls didn't confess and nobody told, but what followed really touched me.

Nikita looked at me, and it was the first time a person ever spoke directly to me as if I mattered! It was almost as if she knew that we were real, too.

"Let's get you straightened up now, yes? You are beautiful, and we are going to fold you just right so you stay happy and pretty all the way to the store tomorrow."

Then Nikita whispered, "Don't tell the others, but *you* are my favorite."

She gently brushed my yarn to straighten me out, placed me on my stomach and folded my arms back in a natural, comfortable position.

"There now, perfect once again," she said with a smile as she placed me back on the shelf.

It was then that I knew what I wanted. I wanted Nikita to be my person.

While I knew that wasn't possible since we were to be shipped off to different stores tomorrow, I thought about how great it would be to get a person just like Nikita. Someone sweet and considerate; and someone who helped me look my best and would make me feel good about who I am. She was perfect, and I felt perfect when she smiled at me.

I also realized that I feel better when I think about what I *do* want instead of focusing on what I do *not* want ... and feeling good is awesome. It occurred to me that if I select my thoughts carefully, I can be much happier and have a much better life.

Tonight was the last night before we're shipped from the warehouse to our stores. Once the workers went home, we all took turns entertaining each other and making promises never to forget each other. For me, it's the songs I will always remember, especially since Michael sang a Christmas song he wrote himself. It was about being away from family on Christmas but still feeling them in your heart. It brought tears to everyone's eyes, especially because of the irony of him not liking Christmas music!

As I fell asleep, I just continued to think about the amazingly wonderful person that would select me. She would be just like Nikita; kind and wonderful ... and we would become best friends.

Sunday, December 8
Dear Diary,

Today was another travel day, and while I am learning to embrace change, I'm also looking forward to a little stability.

When the people arrived at 6:55 am, the lights went on and everyone went right to work. I heard the word "deadline" shouted several times by a couple of people. I think when they said deadline they meant hurry up. What a strange word, *deadline*.

Nikita, our family's worker (and my personal savior), went through the doorway down the hall and came back a few minutes later with some papers in her hand. She then went into the lunchroom and came back with a round ceramic mug in the other. I've learned they call it "having coffee."

Once at her desk, Nikita pulled the first sheet of paper from the pile. She went to the wall on the far side of the warehouse. After briefly deliberating, she selected the appropriately sized box and returned to the desk. She then picked up the paper and started selecting sweaters from the shelf.

It seemed that she was taking one or two of each size from all the sweater families, so the box had at least one of every size and type. Then she put a long, clear strip of plastic across the box, which held it together. "Taping it up" was what they called it at the factory. Then, after grabbing the next piece of paper in the pile to the right, she peeled off a label, placing it on the box. Finally, she placed the box in a large cart, where other boxes were being neatly stacked in different piles by the other workers.

Everything seemed to be happening so fast. We knew we were going to the stores to be matched up with our forever person, but we didn't get a chance to say goodbye today. Somehow, there was that feeling of oneness that I knew we all had in common, and it felt good to think of the memories we would always keep with us … telling jokes, singing and just being together.

When Nikita picked me up to place me in my box, I'm sure she lingered just a moment, as she gently brushed my yarn. Yes, I definitely wanted my forever person to be just like her!

Though I could not see what was going on after the box was closed, I knew we were in one of the "completed" stacks. There were different stacks piled up based on the destination of those boxes. I could smell the savory aroma of the food coming from the cafeteria, so I know we were not put on the trucks until after lunch.

Can you tell how much I am learning? Since we cannot talk or communicate in any way while people are around, we sweaters do a lot of listening. It's amazing how much you learn when you really listen!

The trip to the store was very uneventful, especially considering what a whirlwind the last week had been. I felt the boxes being moved. I felt the truck start to shimmy as it roared to life. I felt the many stops and starts of the truck at first; then, as the sounds of the city grew quiet, there was just a steady, mild vibration that seemed to lull me into a sense of tranquility.

None of the sweaters had much to say. I think we were all just taking it in; at least, I know I was. I thought it would be nice to just enjoy the fact that I was doing nothing for now. After all, we had only heard rumors of what it would be like when we got to the store. I had been thinking of how wonderful it was going to be, and how my perfect forever person would find me as soon as they took me out of the box. My sister Patricia kept repeating the stories about not being picked and getting stuck on the clearance rack. We all heard what happened to clothes on the clearance rack, and it wasn't pretty. I didn't dare even think of it!

For now, I was going to focus on this wonderfully calming ride, and reflect with gratitude on all that had been given to me in my short life.

I'm not sure what time it was when we were taken off the truck and put in the back of our store, but there wasn't a lot of noise so I think the store was closed. I heard it got very busy and very noisy at the stores from the second they opened until after they closed to shoppers; and the closer it got to Christmas, the louder and crazier it got. Which is why my Christmas wish was for my forever person to find me right away.

While the boxes were being taken off the truck, we could hear music being played. They were not songs about Christmas, and the singers seemed to be very angry about something. You could tell because they were screaming, almost as if they were in pain.

In between songs, someone would talk, announcing the song names, and the singer or band. I wasn't sure what the song *Bathing in Mud* was all about, because I couldn't understand the guy from Midnight's Minions, but he clearly was warning you off of his experience. DJ Rick, the man who spoke between songs, called the names of the bands whose music he just played. Shock Monkey, Don't Tase Me Bro, and Gentle

Nightmare. The DJ called them "Metal's finest", and I decided that my forever person should never play this music! Not judging, just sayin'!

Our boxes aren't going to be opened tonight, so sweet dreams. I need my beauty rest!

Monday, December 9
Dear Diary,

My worst nightmare came true. I don't even know where to begin.

It was all his fault. He ruined me and I will never be the same. I am tainted and torn, and I will never be loved again. I am not worthy of love.

I know you think I am being melodramatic, but it is the truth. Here's what happened Diary!

First thing this morning, we were taken out of our boxes and placed on hangers. Next, they attached little pieces of paper to us with our stock number (or SKU) and our price. Each item in this big store has its own SKU number. But I am getting off track; I don't really want to think about what happened to me or what will surely be my resulting fate.

A young boy told another worker he was getting us "floor ready" before placing us on circular clothes racks out in the main store. I have to say, I was awestruck at first by the store's amazing size. In all my two weeks on earth, I had never seen anything like it. It took me all day to get to know the names of things. I listened closely to the people walking through the store, talking about the "merchandise."

We were in the middle of the women's clothes area. There were other sweaters, shirts, jackets, pants, pajamas – thousands of beautiful choices all in one place. Across the aisle were purses and scarfs, and behind them was sparkling jewelry hanging from displays, while other items were being shown inside glass cubes. The jewelry really held my attention. All that sparkle and bling! That's why I wasn't paying attention when he walked up behind me.

This large, short boy with red freckles all over his face grabbed me off the rack and held me up above his head.

"Check this one out," he bellowed.

I didn't get a good vibe from him at all. I was clearly several sizes too small for him.

He brought me over to a girl who was more my size and he started pulling on my poms ... hard!

"Look at these," he said as he chuckled in a weird, unpleasant way. Then he started pulling my poms even harder and asked her if she liked them.

Then it happened. He pulled one of my poms right off me! The pain was unbearable and I almost blacked out.

"Now you've done it. You ruined the sweater," said the girl. "Get rid of it. Nobody's going to want it now."

Through the pain where my pom had been viciously ripped from me, I could feel a deeper pain. What did she mean *nobody would want me*? I was still the same. It wasn't my fault I had been injured. My pom could be reattached!

I was feeling embarrassed, just like at the warehouse when the three girls were calling me ugly and taking pictures of each other while wearing me. The combination of being scared, humiliated and hurt was making me a little sick to my stomach.

Adding further insult to injury, the buffoon tossed my pom on the floor and stuck me between the other sweaters on the rack. I was not put back on a hanger; I was not folded nicely. I was just hidden so he wouldn't get in trouble for being mean to me. My only solace was in knowing that I wouldn't be stuck going home with him due to the store's "you-break-it-you-buy-it" policy. Nobody saw him "break" me.

I looked over at the jewelry, but it didn't seem to sparkle as bright as it had only a scant few moments before. I felt so cheapened by the abuse of that boy that I couldn't enjoy the kids, or the laughter, or the spirit of Christmas; that is, until just before closing. What I saw and heard then changed everything.

I saw a young woman pushing her child in a small pink wheelchair. The young girl looked to be about six years old in people years. She had dark beautiful hair and bright green eyes, along with the cutest pink cheeks. The mother was clearly looking for Christmas deals, as she turned every price tag before taking any item off the rack for a better look.

An elderly man with a cane came hobbling along. He was in a hurry and not paying attention to what was going on around him. As he hurried past the mother and daughter, his cane ran into the little girl's leg and she let out a muffled cry. This startled the old man, and once the look of surprise cleared his face it was replaced by hostility.

"Where did you come from?" he barked at the little girl. "You need to watch where you are going." Then to the mother, "If she

43

is going to be in one of those things, you better teach her how to use it. What kind of a mother are you?"

"Excuse us, sir. We will be more mindful in the future," was the woman's gentle reply.

Not quite satisfied but left with nothing to say, the old man retreated, cane in hand and grumbling under his breath.

Once he was far enough away, the little girl looked up at her mother, confused and wanting answers.

"Why was he so mean to me?" she asked. "Did I do something wrong that I don't understand? He really did bump into me, mommy. Why did you apologize? I don't know what I did wrong, but I must have done something because I sure feel bad."

I wanted to reach out and tell her that it was not her fault, that she had no reason to feel bad. And as this urge got stronger, I realized that this was good advice for me, too. It wasn't my fault that a boy had been mean to me earlier, either. The only difference was that I had to worry about never being picked by a forever person and the little girl had a mom.

But I know I'll never forget what the little girl's mother told her in response to the very valid questions.

The woman squatted down so she was eye level with her chair-ridden daughter.

"I am glad you are asking, Elizabeth. You see, when someone else is in a bad mood or wants to be mean, their energy level is vibrating very low. When people are happy and friendly to others, their energy level is vibrating very high. Does that make sense so far?"

44

Little Elizabeth considered the answer with a scrunched-up face, then replied in a tone that was low and slow, "So when people are upset, they are looow and slooow." Then Elizabeth's voice got excited and she took on a higher, quicker tone, "and when people are in a good mood they are high and happy?"

Her mother smiled and nodded, "I think you have that part right. Now consider this. If a person is looow and slooow," she said, mimicking Elizabeth's earlier tone, "then perhaps it is because something has happened to them that is making them sad. Maybe they are sick or afraid of something. There are many reasons why people can get looow and slooow. Do you think we can be kind enough not to judge them, and instead show them the Christmas spirit no matter what time of year it is?"

Elizabeth broke out in a big smile, "Of course, mommy. We should be extra nice to everyone all the time, especially if they are being mean, right?"

"Right," her mother answered. "However, there are a couple of other things to keep in mind. First, it is important that you keep your own energy vibrating high. This is what keeps you safe and happy in life. So when someone says or does something that is coming from a low or negative place, the only way they can take you to that negative place, too, is if you start thinking negative thoughts about what they did."

She continued. "When the man first bumped you, it may have hurt a little where he bumped you, but inside, you still felt okay, yes?"

Elizabeth thought a moment and responded, "Yes."

"When did you start feeling bad inside?" her mom queried.

"When he started yelling at me," replied Elizabeth. "I got very upset. I wondered how anyone could bump into me and then turn around and yell at me. *He* should have apologized to *me*!"

"So you started to feel bad when you started to have bad thoughts about his behavior."

"Yes," Elizabeth said with a bit of annoyance, "He was rude."

"And when you stop thinking those thoughts and start thinking that maybe he just got bad news, or could be sick ... and you begin feeling compassion for the man, how do you feel?"

Elizabeth took a second to immerse herself in imaginary compassion for the man and you could see her mood change. "I feel better, mom."

"And the lesson here, my precious Elizabeth, is this: You cannot change what other people will say or do. But realize that when someone is being mean or belittling you, it is all about what they are going through – which has nothing to do with you. When you reach out in compassion, even when you are not being treated with the same respect, you will always know you did your best. And when you keep your thoughts on feelings like love and compassion, you have a superpower. It's like an invisible force field blocking any negative energy from putting you in a bad mood.

"And no matter what anyone says or does to you," the mother continued, "that does not change the kind, pretty, funny, future artist that you are. Never think that you are less than perfect because of what someone else says or does! Understand?"

"I understand, mommy," said Elizabeth as she leaned forward and threw her arms around her mother's neck.

46

As her mother stood back up and start wheeling Elizabeth away, I found myself smiling, too. This was exactly what I needed to hear; exactly when I needed to hear it. I was going to be compassionate about the mean boy who pulled off my pom. Maybe his mother dropped him on his head when he was a baby; or maybe he drank cleaning fluid as a kid. But I now knew that I was still wonderful, and the right person would see that. I would find a forever home no matter what the brain-damaged person had done to me.

I also realize that perhaps I still need to work on this compassion thing, but it's a start.

Tuesday, December 10
Dear Diary,

I had a feeling when I woke up that today was going to be the day. It seems like I have been imagining this day forever, and it was better than anything I could have wished for.

When the store opened, customers flooded in. People rarely came into the area with the Christmas sweaters, but when they did, it seemed like they picked up every sweater to take a good look. I love the way they would laugh as they compared sweaters. One customer held up a girl from the "Kittens in the Stockings" sweater family, while her friend held up a boy from the "Garland Tree" sweater family. Then they both broke out in fits of laughter.

They acted like they were treasure hunting and had just found gold. The playful atmosphere was wonderful. People were taking their time in our section, unlike the rest of the store, where everyone seemed to be in a hurry.

With the words of the mother from yesterday still ringing in my ears, I was feeling good. This was a perfect day. I was perfect in my own way, and I would find the perfect forever person for me. I had heard that Christmas sweaters are only worn during one month of the year. In my mind, my forever person would wear me all the time. I was optimistic and feeling good.

My ability to keep my "good vibration" or stay happy was soon to be tested. I had to keep repeating to myself, *don't take things personally*, to get me through it.

A young boy was having a great time looking over all the sweaters in the Christmas section while his mother was browsing through the scarves across the aisle. He was laughing and having fun. I instantly liked him.

I heard the boy squeal with delight as he found the sweater he wanted and tried it on. He was two racks away from me, but clearly it was love at first sight. I realized I didn't care that he hadn't even me a chance. I didn't think a boy was a good match for the life I wanted to lead. It was important to consider those things when you are looking at a forever person. A boy would want to play outside more than a girl and according to the TV shows I had watched, they get dirtier too. My sister Patricia is more of the tomboy type and would've been a perfect match for the boy, but they sent her to a different store.

He ran over to his mom and began repeating, "Mom, mom, mom, mom, mom," while jumping up and down alongside her in an effort to draw her gaze from the scarves that had her attention.

The grin on the boy's face got larger as his mother turned to look at his sweater. Her eyes grew to the size of saucers and her face reddened slightly as she demanded that he take the sweater off immediately and put it back.

The boy protested only a little, clearly knowing that he had crossed a line as he skipped back to the rack to return the sweater. When I saw the sweater he returned, I chuckled a little, too. It was one from the "Santa Bending Over" family. Because you could see a little of his butt while he bent over, it was designed for older people. The R-rated sweater was no match for the boy. I think he just wanted to startle his mother. If that was his objective, it certainly worked!

The boy kept moving down the Christmas sweater aisle. When he stopped in front of me, he smiled and removed me from my hanger, trying me on. It was a pretty good fit, even if I was still not convinced he would provide the right home for me.

He then skipped back over to his mother, who had moved on to the costume jewelry. He cleared his throat twice before she looked his way and grinned. It made me feel good.

"Now that is much better," she said firmly, smiling her approval.

But just as suddenly as her smile appeared, it morphed into a scowl as she noticed my missing pom. She leaned down and picked at the empty spot where the pom once rested, then rose back to full height, clucking pure disapproval.

"You've picked a damaged sweater. Didn't you notice?" she said. "Go find one that isn't falling apart. You'll be tearing it up soon enough. We don't want to start off with one that is messed up from the get-go."

Wow, those words stung at first ... until I remembered the day before.

This woman was not as smart as the mother of the little girl in the wheelchair, and I knew I had value even if the boy's mom did not see it. When I thought about it, I decided I was granted a miracle by not being picked by that family, especially the way she was talking about the boy tearing up his clothes. That was not a life I would have liked.

I would not think about what they said because that would not make me feel good. Instead, I would focus on watching how people were dressed, the looks on their faces when they found the perfect gift for someone, and the upbeat Christmas music. I would think about the great times I had experienced in my life, and feel appreciation for all I had and all that would be coming. And I would look toward the future with excitement and gratitude because I knew it was going to be wonderful.

One of the night cleaners at the factory made a habit of turning on the stereo while he cleaned. He listened to Abraham-Hicks, Deepak Chopra and *The Science of Getting Rich*. I learned a lot about a rule called the Law of Attraction. So I decided to practice some of the things they spoke of, focusing on what I wanted in my home. I began to think about my deep feelings of gratitude for the perfect life waiting for me. I was in a great mood when my forever person showed up. Her name, I later found out, was Katlin. She is mostly called Katie though.

I heard her before I saw her. I noticed a soft, lovely voice humming along with the song playing over the intercom. My first thought was that we would harmonize well together. When she came into sight, I was excited to see that she was just my size – and she had a pleasant face that seemed kind, with golden-colored hair and green eyes.

My heart sank a few seconds later. She decided to try on a baby blue sweater from the Superb Snowflakes family over the shirt she was wearing. She pulled it over her head, grabbed her purse from her cart and walked over to the mirror. She smiled, pleased, checking the fit from multiple angles. She walked back to the rack, still smiling, removed the sweater, put it back on the hanger and placed it in her cart.

I was so sure that the connection I felt meant she was supposed to be my forever person, and now I was feeling a little bad. I was disappointed. Several other people had been down my aisle and I was glad they hadn't selected me … but Katie was different.

She kept walking down the row, closer and closer to me. I wondered if she could feel how bummed I was. Suddenly, she stopped right in front of me and gave me a huge smile.

"Excellent," she exclaimed, startling me a little. She quickly tried me on, and without even looking in the mirror she put me back on the hanger and into the cart. It never occurred to me that she would want two sweaters!

As she took the other sweater out of the cart and put it back on the rack where it originally rested, my elation soared. She picked *me*. It happened so fast but my forever person, Katie, picked me and I was ecstatic!

I was flying high on a cloud when we got to the checkout stand. Katie gently folded me and placed me on the conveyor belt, finding a clean spot to place me on so I wouldn't get dirty. How thoughtful! As I rode to the front of the belt, the cashier grabbed me and pulled my sleeve to get to my tag. She scanned me, and before putting me in the bag she held me up to examine me.

No, no, no!!!

"Excuse me, this sweater is damaged," said the cashier to Katie. "Do you still want it, or do you want to see if there is another one like it?"

Rats! Why couldn't the cashier just mind her own business? My heart sank as I thought of my future on the clearance rack.

"Nope, I'll take this one," was Katie's reply.

What? *Really*?

The cashier persisted, "But I can send someone to see if there is another sweater in the same size."

Seriously, didn't you hear her say she would take me?

I didn't want to spend the day in the returns pile, and I was really sure I was meant to be connected with this person. I wish this tattooed, nose-pierced, too-much-black-eyeliner-wearing cashier would just zip her pierced lip!

"Really, it's fine. I am good with sewing so I can fix her up. I'll keep this one."

Yes, yes, yes!

I held my breath as the cashier replied, "Whatever," and continued ringing the rest of the gifts my person selected while shopping. I was in the bag. *Almost home; my forever home.* I wondered what my new home would be like.

When we got to the house, all the bags of things she purchased at the store were brought into the house and left on the sofa, while she went to another room and made dinner. It smelled really good. I was happy just resting on top of a nice pair of sweatpants and socks in the large plastic bag, and enjoying the aroma of home cooked food.

During this lull of contentment, I heard the front door open and close again. Heavy footsteps passed by the sofa and got softer and softer as they traveled past.

"Where are you?" a male voice called.

"In the kitchen. Just putting dinner on the plate," was my forever girl's reply.

I heard his footsteps as they echoed toward the direction of the kitchen. The two had dinner and that's when I learned, from their conversation, that her name is Katie and his is Ron. They have a dog named Rocky and they like to travel. They meditate every day and do something called yoga.

After dinner, Katie came and got me. Of all the clothes in all the bags, again, she selected me. *Did I tell you, this has been the best day of my life?*

She took me out of the bag, put me on and went in to the room where Ron was reading an article in a magazine.

"Just modeling my Christmas sweater … do you like?"

"Yeah, it's cute," he said.

"Well tomorrow I will get started with Operation Christmas Sweater," she replied. After that she took me off and placed me in a large room with a sewing machine and lots of organizational drawers, where all kinds of arts and crafts items were being stored. There were glues and glitters. There were colored papers and beads. It was sparkly, and I loved this room.

I kind of thought I would be put in a closet, and wondered what she meant by Operation Christmas Sweater. These were my last thoughts as I drifted off to sleep.

Wednesday, December 11
Dear Diary,

Another glorious day. I'm going to a party! Actually, I am going to be *the star* of the party. I know … I tend to get ahead of myself when I'm excited. I'll slow down and go back to the start.

When Katie first entered the craft room today, it was already afternoon. She picked me up and brought me out into the big room that I rested in last night while she made dinner.

I got a better look at the room in the daytime. The area was lit up by the sunshine that cascaded in from a big picture window. It was a bright sunny day, and it smelled nice in here; not like food, but a soft vanilla smell. I think it came from the fragrant, pretty candles that were aglow with life.

She placed me on the sofa, and reached for a pad of paper and a pen. Much to my surprise, she started talking to me.

"You are going to be the belle of the ball, the hit of the party, my dear. You are already awesome and we are going to dress you up! This is your first party, and I know you want to look good, don't you?"

"Yes!" I shouted loudly (in my mind), "I *do* want to look good for my first party!"

While I wanted to scream "yes" out loud, I remembered the number-one rule I was taught the very first day I was created: we do not talk when people are present in the room. I was just so excited to be here and listen to her tell me how awesome I am. It felt really good to have someone tell me they appreciate me.

She continued her one-sided conversation, running through a list of all the decorations and jewelry I would be adorned with once she was finished with me.

"First, I think we need lights."

She wrote something on a notepad, and then turned her attention back to me.

"Where to put the lights ..." she pondered. "We will try to get them on your tree. Your tree will look good with lights."

She moved over to a device with a monitor and a keyboard that had letters scattered all over it, and started typing. When she hit the "enter" key, the monitor was filled with pictures of mini lights. She did this several times, and each time she pressed "enter" another picture magically appeared. While she was typing away to find lights, I wanted to jump up and down with joy. I was going to light up like Rudolph. Everyone loves a light-up sweater!

"Excellent. They sell it locally. That goes on tomorrow's to-do list," she said. She wrote something on a new piece of paper and looked back at me, smiling.

"What else? Hmmm, maybe some garland. Yes, that will be perfect. And I know where to get that, too. And how about mini ornaments or bigger poms?" she mused.

She then focused her attention back on the machine, tapping away at the keyboard and viewing screen after screen. There were mini ornaments that looked just like the ones on the big tree I saw the day I modeled. The poms seemed to come in all sizes and colors. I liked the poms; but of course I would be partial to them!

"And we are going to put mini presents under your tree, too," she assured me. "You are going to look fantastic! You will be the prettiest sweater at the party! Everyone will be wearing their Christmas sweater and I will have the coolest, best-looking one there. You are going to be smoking hot, young lady."

You know I was beaming, soaking in the praise and so grateful for where I was, with the perfect forever person for me. I was wondering how life could get any better when I overheard Katie on a phone call.

Now don't judge me. She was right next to me and it's not like she was whispering. I wasn't eavesdropping. I could only hear what she was saying but it went something like this.

"It's going to be so much fun. It's on Christmas Eve at Wendy's house. Everyone is going to wear their sweater and we each kick $5 into a pot. Everyone gets one vote and the sweater that gets the most votes wins the money in the pot for its owner. I *know* Sophie and I are going to win."

I stopped listening for a moment as I felt stunned. *How did she know my name*? She just called me "Sophie" and I'm sure our names were not on our tags!

I was pulled back into the conversation when I heard Katie say, "She is going to be the best sweater there. I have lights, and now

I just need to figure out a way to get sound and maybe some special effects going on."

I liked the sound of her laugh. I love how excited she was about the party and spending time dressing me up. I wasn't sure what "special effects" were, but they sounded awesome!

I felt like I was living a charmed life. I was selected to be in an advertisement. I had been chosen by a wonderful person, and we were going to a party where I would be dressed up and entered in a contest on Christmas Eve.

Just to be worn on Christmas Eve was an honor. If you were worn on Christmas Day, that was the biggest honor, with Christmas Eve being a close second. I've made the big time!

I wasn't sure how many days it was until Christmas Eve and I didn't really care. I was glad just to be having fun. That night as I fell asleep, the thought floated through my head … how can it get any better?

Thursday, December 12
Dear Diary,

You should know that beauty has a price.

Today is the day that lights were to be added to my tree.

Before we got started, Katie put me on and tried to take a "selfie" of me. Her arms are too short and you couldn't see me in the picture, so she took me off and laid me flat on her bed. She smoothed out the bedspread and gently flattened me so I had no wrinkles. She used her phone to take a couple pictures. She looked at them and didn't seem satisfied. She turned on all the lights in the room and took another photo. She was pleased this time, so she took a couple more and then moved my arms so it looked like I was posing with attitude. It seems my girl has a sense of humor!

Once she got all the "before" pictures, we moved to the big room. I quickly locked my attention onto a plastic bag. Hanging out of it were the same miniature lights we saw when she was shopping on her computer yesterday. I heard her refer to it as a "laptop" when she was talking to Ron.

After being thoroughly examined, Katie determined that my yarn was too thick to just push the lights through and have them pop up on my tree, so she needed to put the string of lights on top of the tree and sew the wires in place.

I appreciated that Katie was good about not sticking me. She carefully weaved the thread between my strings of yarn rather than through them. After about five minutes, I learned I could trust her and relax – and enjoy my transformation.

She would bring each light to the place she wanted, and then use the needle to pull the thread through the opening and tie it off. She would then repeat the process of pulling the thread through the yarn and the light string until she seemed sure it would stay in place. After that, she would triple-knot the end so it was tight and secure.

She continued doing the same thing for every light for the next 15 minutes, and then she held me up in the air. She stared at me for a long time, expressionless. Finally, she took a deep breath in and exhaled, shaking her head.

She got up and returned with small pair of scissors. Being very precise, she cut each of the series of threads that were wrapped around the tiny lights.

I was hoping she would talk to me and tell me what she was thinking, and what she intended to do next. I knew that I couldn't change any of her choices, but I felt like I was more in control when I knew what was going on. Weird, huh?

"Just too long in between," was all I heard her mutter.

Over the course of the next hour, she found some green floral tape in a drawer and sat down with the lights. She folded the wire between the first and second light three times so that it was shorter, then used the floral tape to hold her alteration together.

This seemed promising at first, but after she folded and wrapped the wire between a dozen or more lights, she realized the tape was not sticking. I listened as she lamented to someone on her phone that she would need green electric tape because the floral tape was not sufficient.

I heard the jingle of her keys, and I saw a blur I'm pretty sure was her as she breezed by me, leaving to go and acquire the special tape. I found it hard to believe that the floral tape wouldn't stick and probably wouldn't believe it had I not seen it. After all, isn't the whole purpose of tape *to stick*? I still remember the calls of the workers in the factory so long ago as they constructed the boxes they put us in. "Tape it up!" Yes, tape was supposed to stick.

When she returned, she went quickly to work. She was intently focused on the task at hand and didn't even answer her cell phone when it rang. It took less than an hour before all the wires were folded over so they were shorter and taped into position. Now she could put the lights on the tree without a bunch of wires all over the place.

She started sewing, and I thought everything was going well. After she tacked down the first five lights, she looked at her progress. The lights were not going on as planned; instead, they seemed to have a life all their own.

Katie's expression indicated that she had resigned herself to the fact that she would need to resort to Plan B, which I have learned always entailed calling her best friend Isabel for advice.

"Okay, so lights on the tree just are not happening. Should I add them to the arm or make a frame around the tree."

Silence … then, "It would have to spiral down the arm," Katie replied to whatever advice she was just given over the phone.

"I could tuck the box with the batteries up my sleeve," offered my person, as if solving a problem.

"Awesome! Come by and see it later," she concluded and put her phone on the table.

It was easy to guess Isabel's advice based on what Katie was saying: The arm it was.

Katie made some hot tea, returned and spent the next 90 minutes sewing the lights down my arm. When she tied the final knot, she opened the back of the battery pack and inserted two AA batteries. She then switched the lights on ... and I was totally lit up.

She gleefully put me on, then ran down the hall to the full-length mirror on the back of the bathroom door. I looked fantastic! This was great. There is something about wearing something special that makes you really feel good ... know what I mean?

Isabel came over and Katie tried me on again. I loved the look on her face when Katie turned the lights on.

"Ta-da!" I shouted silently to myself.

When Ron came home, he said we might be able to find smaller lights for the tree, too. Katie said she liked me this way, but if she finished giving me my makeover and I still needed a little pizzazz, she would look into it.

If I feel this good when I only have lights added, I wonder how good I'm going to feel when I'm totally dolled up?!

I love my life!

Friday, December 13
Dear Diary,

I love garland. It's so glittery and flashy and tickly. I'm so happy with my new bling that I don't even care what Isabel said, although it was rude.

It was afternoon again when Katie came into the craft room. She picked me up and put me over her arm, and then went to the corner where there was a big plastic bag. She grabbed the bag and a sewing kit, and the next thing I knew we were headed out to the living room. Today, she turned on the television while she dressed me up. She decided on a show called *Oprah's Life Lessons*.

The show was a rerun, and Oprah was talking to a woman who had studied the psychology of success. She could train a person's mind to think in a way that allowed them to have everything they wanted in life. When she talked, it sounded so easy.

She had a book and a program called *Train Your Brain for Rock Star Success*. I loved the way she explored not only what to do, but how she set it up with a step-by-step process on how to do it. It was broken down into a formula anyone could follow. I couldn't see the television, but it all sounded like great advice, and I wished I could learn more from the woman.

My forever girl had the candles lit and it smelled like cinnamon. It was a great day.

Katie weaved the garland back and forth across my tree, making it look as if it had been strung across the trees limbs. She carefully stitched each edge of the arch, making sure not to poke my yarn. Once she was done, she held me up and smiled with delight. She put me on and ran to the mirror.

"Yes! Perfect," she exclaimed. "But …"

She ran back to the living room, peeling me off as she went. I got turned inside out and she reversed me as she sat down. Grabbing a piece of garland, she ran it along the bottom of my sleeve. When one end touched the other, she removed it and cut it – just a little longer than needed. Then she cut a second piece of garland the same length.

Over the next 45 minutes, she sewed the strips of garland along the cuffs of my sleeves. No question, it did look pretty cool. It was gold garland and really bright. Maybe I *would* win this contest!

When she finished there was more garland left, and it seems Katie doesn't like to waste. She took another long strip and wrapped it around the neck, cutting it to be just longer than needed to make the full circle … and she sewed that on, too. I have to admit it was a nice touch.

There were two shorter pieces I thought would be left for scrap. Did I mention that Katie doesn't like to leave anything unused? She sewed the leftover garland around my bottom. It took both pieces, and there was still a two-inch gap where there was nothing on the side.

I don't mean to be blunt, but it looked stupid.

I knew Katie wouldn't leave me looking like that – and she didn't. She found a large pink velvet bow and sewed it on.

I'm not sure how I feel about the bow. She never mentioned a bow or garland around the cuffs, collar or bottom. Oh well, what's one more adjustment in my ever changing life?

Isabel came over after dinner, and I heard them talking in the other room. They were laughing and I felt a little left out. I wanted them to come in and see me. I wondered what Isabel would think of my makeover so far.

I could smell he savory aroma of something so good wafting into the room. Even though I don't eat, I really appreciate the smell of good food.

As if reading my mind, the door to the craft room opened, and Katie excitedly grabbed me. "Close your eyes until I tell you to open them, Issa!" Katie shouted. She hurriedly put me on, taking care not to mess up any of my new decorations.

When I was on properly, Katlin slid over to the mirror, sliding on her socks. She took a quick look and headed to the living room.

"Okay, open."

Isabel sat there, speechless. My lights were flashing, and the garland was shimmering as the track lights on the ceiling caused it to shine. She must have been blinded by my awesomeness.

After several long moments, Issa lost it, laughing uncontrollably. "OMG, that is great. That is the coolest ugly sweater I have ever seen! You look like total trailer trash."

I knew it. She loved it. I was amazing. The coolest....

What was that? Did she say *ugly sweater*? But she was acting as if she liked me. I was very confused and it didn't feel good. I wasn't sure whether I should be flattered or angry. And what is trailer trash? I thought trash meant garbage.

I tried to remember the lesson I learned in the store about not taking things personally and if someone is mean it is their problem and not yours. But why did it keep coming up that I was ugly? I didn't feel ugly, and people acted like they loved me. I was very perplexed.

"Do you like?" Katie asked.

"Like it? I love it!" Isabel exclaimed.

I must have heard wrong. Issa came up and brushed against my garland and laughed at my lights.

"That sweater will definitely win," declared Isabel.

"Yeah, and I'm not done yet!" announced Katie.

While they were both acting like I was the best thing that ever happened to either one of them, I was getting a feeling of foreboding I did not like one little bit.

Katie took me off and put me back in the craft room. I decided not to think about Issa'a hurtful words and that it was time to escape to the sweet bliss of dreamland. Sweet dreams, diary.

Saturday, December 14
Dear Diary,

I've been in a much better mood all day long. I'm not sure what was wrong with me yesterday, but I realized if I could just think happy thoughts, I would be happy. It really works.

A couple times I started to slip into a bad mood, and as soon as I noticed it, I asked myself what I had just been thinking about. All three times, I was thinking about something that someone said or did that wasn't nice to me. Then I decided to make an effort to think about my great home, the nice people I had met, and all the things I had accomplished in my life (being a model for a newspaper ad was kind of a big deal, you know), and I felt so much better. I even had a party and a contest to look forward to. When I thought about it, life really doesn't get much better and I wanted to be appreciative and happy. It just felt better.

I heard Katie tell Isabel last night that if you want to get out of a bad mood in under 60 seconds to go to a mirror, look at yourself and smile. Within 15 seconds your whole demeanor will brighten and you will snap right out of it. You can continue smiling at yourself for the remainder of the 60 seconds and get in a really good mood. Sometimes people start getting in a good mood and they stop smiling at themselves before the 60 seconds and walk away from the mirror. Apparently, there are some times when a person just doesn't want to be in a good mood.

Wanting to be angry or upset didn't make sense to me, but the more people I met, the more I saw people who seemed to be that way. Luckily, though, not all of them were like that. I wondered if the smiling-in-the-mirror thing worked for sweaters, too? There wasn't a mirror in the craft room so I couldn't try it.

I don't know where the woman found them, but when she brought me out of my room and into the living area, there were these adorable miniature ornaments on the table. They looked just like the round shiny ones you put on a life-sized tree, and there was glitter wrapped around each ball. I just knew these were for me, and I was feeling like every day was Christmas, and each day I received a new gift.

I had also heard about another holiday called Hanukah that happened this time of year. Maybe I was getting Hanukah gifts, too. I don't really care what we're celebrating; I just like how people seem to have more fun and are nicer to each other when it's a holiday. Sometimes, things just feel right, and people being kind and considerate of each other felt very right.

We watched a Christmas movie on the Hallmark channel as Katlin hand-stitched each ornament firmly to the front of my tree. The movie was about a woman who went home for the holidays because of an ailing parent, after being gone for 10 years. She ran into her old boyfriend, whom she left behind when she headed for the city life, wanting to be free of the small minds in the small town. Sparks were ignited, but were quickly doused when her fast-talking, city slicker fiancé flew in at the last minute to be with her for the holiday.

When a big deal pulled the fiancé away on Christmas Eve, the ghost of Christmas future came to show her what her life with Mr. Wheel 'n Deal would be like. She realized she didn't want that, and she broke it off with him.

The heartbroken-for-a-second-time high school boyfriend is cajoled by the girl's sick mom to come over and fix the heater that had conveniently broken, with a little help from the previously mentioned sick mom, of course, on Christmas Day. While he was fixing the heater, the mother let it slip that the love of his life (her daughter) had just become available.

While the end didn't reveal whether they ended up together, it was implied when, hand in hand, they mounted a snowmobile and rode off to a beautiful frozen pond. The final scene showed them staring into each other's eyes where, lost in the moment, they kissed and the camera faded to black.

It was a great afternoon; one of the best ever. Katlin drank hot cocoa and added ornaments to me while we watched a movie.

But what came next was really flippin' awesome: they put up a Christmas tree! Now I know this may not seem like a big deal since this is a tradition many families participate in every year, but it's a huge deal for me. I had never seen the way one is assembled. It takes planning and teamwork. Some tasks are separate, while others are done in a synchronistic dance.

First, the tree wasn't real; that was my first shocker. Ron pulled in this big box that was stored in what they call an attic. It sounded like that is where they keep things that they don't use all year long. Since I had heard that Christmas sweaters are not worn all year long, the thought crossed my mind that she could put *me* in the attic! I decided not to dwell on that thought and just enjoy the activity going on in front of me.

Next they brought out about 20 to 25 smaller boxes ... and then it was show time! I watched, fascinated, as they constructed the tree. All the branches had snow on one of the ends; remarkably, the snow didn't come off. On the other end was a thick metal wire with a color on its tip. They started by making piles of branches, a different pile for each color on the end of the metal tip.

Once they had all the branches in their proper piles, it was easy to see that the colors represented the different sizes of the branches. This made sense. It would look stupid if there were large branches at the top and small ones at the bottom and all different sizes all over the place. Well, maybe it would look kind of cool, but they had a goal to make this fake foliage look like a respectable Christmas tree ... and they did!

One by one each branch was placed, starting at the bottom. When they got about shoulder high, a large mini tree made of the same materials as the other individual branches, was hoisted to the middle of the pole. The thick metal wire from the bottom of the mini tree was inserted into a hole in the pole, into which all the other branches were inserted. This completed the look of a mighty fir that might have been found deep in the forest.

Lights were next, and there was some debate over the best way to hang them. I thought maybe this was their first Christmas together since they did not have a system, and I was glad to be part of it.

"How do you usually put the lights on? It *is* all about the lights on a Christmas tree. That will make or break the whole look, you know," Katie, said looking over at Ron with an impish smile.

I knew it. It was our first Christmas together!

"If we start at the top," Ron was saying, "and just criss-cross back and forth instead of wrapping all the way around the whole tree, it will be faster and easier to take them off after Christmas. And nobody is going to see the back of the tree since it's against the wall."

The man had a valid point.

"I see what you mean, and I do like fast and easy. But will it look as good? By going all the way around, the lights will shine through from behind, and I would really like our first tree to be perfect; wouldn't you?" Katie asked as she leaned in to kiss him.

He agreed with her, so round and round went the lights.

He was slow and deliberate as he added the lights. Katie leaned in to watch, and asked what he was doing.

"Well, since we want the tree to be perfect … for our perfect first Christmas … I'm taking the time to weave the lights around the branches so the wires will be hidden."

He received a big smile from Katie. She was clearly pleased that he took to heart her request for making the tree look good. She watched and repeated his actions when she took the lights. Back and forth, one would weave the lights carefully on one side of the tree, then reach around to give the other person the ball of lights so they could take their turn. After a long time, they finally reached the bottom and the lights were plugged in. It was spectacular! There were only a few lights that were not working, and they were on the last strand of lights.

"Next time, let's remember to plug in each set of lights *before* we add them to the tree," Ron suggested.

"Great idea," Katie replied. "Thankfully it's the last row, not the ones at the top."

"I love how you always see the bright side of things," Ron said as he pulled her close and gave her another kiss.

I was blushing a little, but they didn't notice.

It looked like they worked well together, and I loved the way they were open to considering each other's suggestions instead of doing what they thought was the best or right way … just because that is how they've done it in the past.

I started thinking they both had the opportunity to learn new things by being open to changing what they already knew. Wow, that was deep!

Back to the tree. After the lights, they draped the garland. It was like the garland on me, but their tree had silver garland, and I had gold. Also, the garland on the tree was much larger than mine. Okay, maybe it wasn't like the garland on me. I wondered how many colors of garland were out there. I thought I had seen red, too, during my brief stay at the department store.

Next, they put on decorations that were all purple, white or silver. They started with the silver and purple balls, purposely alternating the colors so there weren't any areas that were covered all by one color. After the ornaments, they added all kinds of tiny musical instruments. They called out the names of some of them as they added them, being silly and pretending to play the tiny miniatures. There were tubas, flutes, pianos, guitars, harps, violins, stand-up bass guitars and more. It was beautiful. After that, they attached glitter-dusted silver bows with pinecones attached.

The last box of ornaments they opened was a mismatch of different items. There was a larger guitar that didn't look like the rest, a baby grand piano, a microphone, the Eiffel Tower, the Coliseum from Rome, the Golden Gate Bridge, and a crystal heart.

Now I know you are thinking I am pretty smart for a sweater because I know about so many places all over the world. Well, I am very smart, but I'll come clean and tell you all of the truth.

I heard them stop and reminisce as they took each ornament out of the box, hanging them one by one. Some of the memories were associated with decorations they owned before they met, while   others were ornaments they acquired together over the last year. I learned that collecting Christmas ornaments was one of the things that had brought them together. They kissed each time they hung a new ornament, recalling the significance of each one. At that point I was thinking "the girl is watching too many Hallmark channel movies!"

They completed the tree decoration with a large silver star on top, and when they plugged in the lights, I was awestruck. With mostly silver, white and purple, the tree was stunning. As the couple stood arm-in-arm looking at the tree, admiring its beauty, I understood how they felt. They had imagined it, and then they brought it to life. That brought them satisfaction, contentment and joy … and even though I didn't do the work, I could see and feel the energy of their pride and happiness, and I felt part of it.

The duo went off to the other room, and when they came back it looked like they had a makeover of their own. She was in a black pant suit with stylish boots. Her shirt was black velvet with red lace sleeves. With her hair pulled tightly back in a ponytail, her large gold hoop earrings stood out. Ron had on a long-sleeve button-up collared shirt, with jeans and dress shoes.

They brought out wine, wine glasses, and a cheese and cracker plate as the doorbell rang, announcing the arrival of two guests. When everyone said their hellos, I learned the name of the guests were Erik and Lisa. You could tell they had been here before since the big German Shepherd, Rocky, just wagged his lengthy tail as if they were long-time friends.

I liked Rocky a lot. He had big black ears and was always smiling. He was playful and fun, unless someone he did not know came to the house. Then he turned into a fierce protector! After his friendly sniffing hello, he wandered over to his favorite spot on the edge of the throw rug, circled three times, and nestled into a ball as he placed his paw over his nose.

The friends were equally impressed with the tree, and I got to hear the story of how it came to life while the four of them were enjoying wine, cheese and each other's company.

Lisa mentioned that she liked using one color for all her tree decorations, and how Katie and Ron's tree looked like it was decorated by a professional in a department store. She went on to say that her tree was a mismatch of ornaments and colors, and asked Katie to share her decorating tips. Katie replied that bringing their Christmas tree to life was "easy as cake and simple as pie," then she laughed.

"That's the acronym I use in my workshops and programs," Katie explained, "and when you use it, you can make cool things happen. Would you like me to tell you my formula, which will also give you a preview of a book I am writing?"

"Yes, definitely," Erik and Lisa chimed in. Ron just grinned. I was guessing she had already shared this formula with him.

"First we decided what we wanted our tree to look like," she explained. "What kind of ornaments, what color garland, how many lights, and so on. We got very clear on what we wanted and exactly what it would look like. The "C" in cake stands for Clarity of your vision. Being crystal clear on what you want is key in making things happen."

"What if I want more money?" Erik asked. His question was greeted with a round of laughter. "I've been very clear on wanting more money; still I'm not retired yet."

"Don't you get a raise every year?" asked Katie.

"A small one," Erik replied.

"Well, you are getting exactly what you are asking for. More money. How much do you want? Give me a number. Be exact."

Erik thought for a second and confessed, "I don't know."

"Decide how much you want down to the penny, and make that amount your focus. Without this first step, getting crystal clear, you won't get what you want. Think of it this way, if you called a travel agent told them you wanted to go on vacation, you would have to tell them where you wanted to go, what day you wanted to leave, how long you were going to stay, what kind of hotel you wanted, and so on.

"Anytime you want to bring something into your existence, you have to get very clear," Katie continued. "The more detail you provide to your imagination, the sooner the universe can find or create it and bring it to you."

"So if I said I want a million dollars?" Erik asked. This time he seemed much more serious as he waited for the answer.

"When do you want it? I mean, by what date? Do you want it in the form of cash in the bank? You want to get as clear as you can on what you want. Just don't concern yourself with how you will get it yet."

"Got it," Erik answered.

"Let's stay with the example of you and your million dollars," Katie explained as she looked at Erik.

"Great idea. Let's talk about me having a million dollars," Erik enthusiastically agreed.

With a smile, Katie pressed on. "The A in cake stands for 'Acting in total faith as if you already have it.' That's the second step."

Seeing the look on Lisa's face Katie jumped right in. "That doesn't mean you go spending it before you have it, Erik," she cautioned knowingly.

Erik crossed his arms in front of him and put on an exaggerated frown, which brought another round of laughs from the group.

"It means being as grateful as you would be if the money were in your bank account now. Imagine how you would feel if your bank statement showed a cool million in the bank … and do your best to continue feeling that way. Believe it or not, being grateful for something to come, as if it is already here, will bring it to you faster," Katie explained.

Ron, Erik and Lisa were all listening intently.

"The K in cake stands for 'Keeping your focus on what you want, while being flexible to how you get it.' And always expect that what you want will become yours and feel deep gratitude.

Expect and be grateful."

"That's all great and I like cake, but how does that help get a project done?" Lisa interjected.

Katie laughed. I noticed that I really liked her laugh. It's light and kind of carefree.

"The cake is the mindset … developing the habit of thinking that way makes it easy and fun to accomplish your goals, but this mindset alone won't do the trick. That's where the 'pie' comes in."

"What kind of pie are you serving tonight," Erik chimed in with a hearty chuckle.

"With any project, goal or dream, bringing it from the mind to the world requires planning and preparation. So the **P** in pie does double duty; it stands for plan and prepare," Katie went on. "Yet that alone is not enough. You also have to **I**mplement those plans. Taking action brings life to your plans. After that, all you have to do is **E**ngage and give 100% to everything you do … and then just watch the magic unfold.

"You just got the very short version of my upcoming book."

"How is the book coming?" Lisa asked.

"Enough about me, I want to find out what you two have been up to," Katie countered, looking at her friends.

The couples continued talking and sharing stories for a bit longer before Erik and Lisa said their goodbyes.

I learned so much from watching my forever couple put up the tree, and even more when their friends came over. It occurred to me that I learned the most by watching how people interact, and by listening to their stories.

What a fun way to remember. Easy as **CAKE,** simple as **PIE**. I think I'm getting hungry. Oh, that's right … I don't eat. It's time for bed, anyway. Sweet dreams.

Sunday, December 15
Dear Diary,

I figured out what my person does for a living today. She said
she was writing a book yesterday, but I did not put everything
together until this morning. She is the one that was on the *Oprah*
show that day. Her big seller is about training your brain to think
in the way that will bring you the results you want … easier, and
with lightning speed.

I heard her talking to her agent, a woman she called Andrea,
about her second book. It was titled, *The Only Guide You Will
Ever Need for Success.* It was broken down in a common-sense,
easy-to-understand format in its synopsis. I listened intently as
Katie read it to Andrea.

Here's the deal. When we are feeling good and our energetic
vibration is high, we are in a creative space where possibilities
are endless; and the right opportunities and the right people
always appear at just the right time. Everything happens to serve
our highest good, which will always be concurrent with the
highest good of all others, as well.

If we are not feeling good, our energetic vibration will be low.
When this happens, we are in a competitive space where we look
at what we don't have … and we feel our opportunities are
limited. This is not true, but because we are not open enough or
vibrating at a frequency that will allow us to see the truth, we
don't see opportunities and possibilities. As a result, we miss

them.

The real truth is that abundance surrounds us, and we can have anything we want when we learn how to use our minds to get it.

Katie went on to explain that we cannot always just change the way we feel, but the way we feel is a direct result of the thoughts we choose to entertain in our minds.

The cool thing is we can change our thoughts. Changing our thoughts will change our mood, and allow us back into that vibrational spot where everything just seems to go our way!

So … my person uses books to send messages to people, so they can train their brain to think in terms of possibilities, and then take the action needed to live the best life possible. Her last book was called *Train Your Brain for Rock Star Success: 5 Musts for Massive Results*. I wondered if she had audio recordings of her books so one day I could listen to all the stuff she shares.

That's why she was home a lot of the time, and Ron was gone most days until dinner. He works on computers.

Today, both were home all day. Ron started early with the outside Christmas decorations. The memo must have gone out in the Neighborhood News, because when I looked out the picture window in the living room where I'd be left, I saw six homes where men were out front with ladders and multiple boxes. It was quite the scene as all the guys gathered in a huddle, discussing what they were planning.

With time, it became evident that two of the neighbors were in a Christmas lights war. After all the wreaths, lights and blow-up lawn ornaments had been secured and brought to life, the tall skinny guy across the street and his next door neighbor, the heavy-set guy with a well-manicured beard, each hopped into their vehicles and left. They both returned an hour later with even more boxes. Tall and Lanky went inside, while Big Guy got to work outside. It was lunchtime before Big Guy finished his labor of love.

After Tall and Lanky peered out and saw Big Guy was finished (he was now standing in the street admiring his overpopulated-even-if-it-was-adorable lawn), he came outside and silently went to work. He started by lengthening his ladder so it went all the way to the roof, and grabbed a large rope. He pulled the boxes out of the bed of his truck, hauling them to the side of the house where, one by one, he tied the rope around a box, took the other end of the rope with him up the ladder ... then used the ladder as a pulley system to get the boxes on his roof. There were five boxes in all, and my eyes were glued to this activity the whole time.

Apparently, I wasn't the only one whose attention was held by this spirited Christmas competition. Slowly, a crowd gathered around Tall and Lanky's house. There was the occasional "Hey," from a neighbor to T and L, but other than that, the neighbors were clearly engaged as mere spectators only. One man came out to water his grass and wandered over to get a better look. A woman came out front with her two kids, and they all gravitated to the action. Soon, there was a small crowd which seemed to pump Tall and Lanky up even further, while Big Guy slowly morphed into Angry Big Guy.

Big Guy hopped back in his SUV and left once more, just before Mrs. Tall and Lanky (who was neither tall nor lanky) came out and offered everyone homemade chocolate chip cookies.

Katie came out of the back room with several small square cubes of Styrofoam, red and green shiny wrapping paper, scissors, glue and small gold string. I wondered what she was up to today as she sat down for today's round of upgrades. But I wasn't going to find out just yet. All the activity going on across the street got her attention, too. T and L was just running all the extension cables down the side of the house and was plugging them in.

Like the zombie film Katie and Isabel watched during their last movie night, all the fabric that had been lying in almost flat piles on the roof began to come to life. I was mesmerized at the transformation, and Katie called to Ron to check out Ed's house as she walked out the front door and joined what was now a crowd across the street. Apparently, Tall and Lanky went by the name of Ed.

Ron followed a few minutes later. Before long, Santa was in a bathtub with Rudolph by his side. I have to say it seemed weird to me that he brought his reindeer in the bathroom with him, but eventually I decided not to think about it anymore.

Next were the snow people (a family of three) in a snow globe. There was also an adorable mouse with big ears on the roof, sitting on the back of a motorcycle with a Santa hat, T-Shirt with rolled-up sleeves, and a tattoo. His female counterpart, a mouse with big eyelashes and a bow in her hair was with him, looking a little trashy in her tight leather jeans, leather jacket and low-cut top. Not judging; just sayin'!

I flashed back to a television commercial I had seen repeatedly during the Hallmark movie, and I could almost hear the voice of the man in the TV ad saying, "But wait, there's more!"

To the right of the Biker Mouse were two gigantic pink flamingos. They were twice as big as the mouse, and the whole thing was screaming *tacky*. Speaking of tacky, on the far right was Santa coming out of a "Porta Potty" … one of those portable bathrooms they put at construction sites. What is it about humiliating Santa that makes people happy? I thought he was the guy with all the gifts! It seems the more I think I know, the less I realize I really do know.

There were oohs and aahs from the street patrol, and T and L couldn't suppress a major grin. The Missus came out and offered him a beer rather than a cookie. It seemed he appreciated that choice, as he guzzled at least half the bottle in one long, smooth pull. His satisfaction was complete when he saw Big Guy roll back into his driveway at the pinnacle of his glory.

As if scripted for a Hollywood movie, Tall and Lanky then turned to the crowd and said, "Merry Christmas y'all; enjoy the view" as he raised his beer bottle. He then maneuvered the empty boxes and ladder into the garage and closed the door, disappearing behind it.

The gathering visited with each other for a short while longer, then slowly dispersed. When Katie returned to the house, she went right back to the task at hand, and I quickly understood what she was up to. She cut the shiny green and red paper and gift-wrapped the little cubes of Styrofoam, putting a dot of glue on each end to hold the paper together instead of Scotch tape like people use on bigger boxes. These little guys were only about an inch cubed, and I could see they were meant for eventual placement under my tree.

I liked the idea of having presents under my Christmas tree and thought it a heartwarming gesture. I fantasized what it would be like to be a human and have this custom. I imagined giving Katie a necklace like one I had seen on one of the models at the photo shoot so long ago. I could see the joy on her face as clearly as if it were happening in front of me at that moment.

Then I thought of all the people in my life who I loved, and who I would buy presents for if I could.

It was fun thinking about giving people things. It felt even better than thinking about people giving me things, though I do like thinking about that, too.

I thought it was a nice tradition.

Once the glue dried, she used the gold string and tied it on the packages so it looked like ribbon. The packages were adorable. Teeny tiny little fake presents; and soon they were under my tree. I was looking good. No, I was looking great! That's right. And I've gotta say, it feels good to look good! Go me ... go me. *Woot, woot!*

It was dark now, and I could smell the food cooking on the barbeque. I'm told being able to barbecue in the winter is one of the perks of living in Florida. Of course, the downside of Florida for a sweater is that we only get to go out when it's cold, which doesn't happen in Florida very much. But I lucked out; my person gets cold all the time, and she's been wearing me a lot! Right now, with the smell of the fish grilling from outside, the aroma of whatever else was cooking coming from the kitchen, the completion of my makeover, feeling good about myself, and not being stuck in a closet all the time, I was loving Florida and loving life. The thought went through my head once more, *how can it get any better?*

I was about to find out.

When the darkness settled in outside, Big Guy's lights went on, and the whole neighborhood was lit up. There were lights around every tree, every shrub ... and seemingly every inch of the front of his house except the windows and garage door.

There were large candy canes along his driveway and sidewalk. They were the same kind of candy canes that acted as a fence surrounding the Gingerbread House on the set of my photo shoot. There were light-up decorations, too, weaved in between the lawn ornaments that covered every inch of his yard. There was a wreath on every window that I could see, and lights around all of his windows and doors.

On his roof he had lights that changed and created different designs to the music that he was now playing loud enough to hear blocks away! The song *Rudolph* was playing, and you could see Rudolph in lights on the roof, prancing around. The Santa appeared in the lights and patted the little reindeer's head. It was fun to watch, and a crowd assembled on the sidewalk once again.

Big Guy was pleased. Tall and Lanky, after watching the show for only 30 seconds, dropped his shoulders, turned and retreated back into his house.

I'm not sure why they were trying to be better than each other. Can't everyone see that we are just different, and our differences are to be appreciated?

But this only saddened me as long as I thought about it, so I turned my thoughts to something that made me happier – like how good I was looking. I bet Katlin wears me all the time now that she has finished me. I can't wait for the party. I wondered how many days until Christmas Eve!

Monday, December 16
Dear Diary,

Today brought many surprises. I am learning that life changes fast, and while it is good to have an idea of what you want, flexibility and patience is important.

I told you how I saw the way Tall and Lanky and Big Guy got a little competitive about the Christmas decorations yesterday. And I've got a pretty good idea that one or both of them will be at the store today looking for more things to clutter their yard, so theirs is the biggest spectacle in the neighborhood. They are not buying things to look pleasing. There is no Gingerbread house with a train set going around it. There is no tastefulness to the Santa images being selected. What once was probably good fun is now a competition that looks and feels bad.

I could accept that behavior from them, but I wondered what was up with my person. She is all miss "coming-from-a-higher-place" with her self-help talk. And I am trying to come from my "higher place" here, but I thought we were done with my makeover. I thought I looked good before what she did to me today. I'm not sure what look she is going for, but I am starting to feel like Tall and Lanky's roof – some kind of freak show! Is this all about the contest? I'm trying to give her the benefit of the doubt, so I'll let you be the judge.

Now I was almost okay with just the bells, and at first that was all I saw on the table. They were loud, noisy bells that made this obnoxious jingling noise when she would pick one up. There were 16 of them on the table before me. That's right … 16 silver, shiny, shrill bells … and don't forget, my garland is gold *so the silver bells totally clash*! But I'm getting ahead of myself. Breathe Sophie, breathe! Connect with your higher self.

Okay, it started first thing in the morning. She came into the craft room and I knew she was either going to make a spot for me in the closet (where I would get to meet everyone else) or she was going to wear me. I thought maybe we might even go outside to do some shopping. Either way, I knew it was going to be my last day in the craft room.

I thought about how I was going to miss this little room. The soft, blue color was very relaxing and I loved all the color that seemed to pop against the pastel background. All the stickers, ribbons, papers, beads, glitter and other craft supplies were a rainbow of colors that were bright, bold and beautiful.

When she tossed me over her shoulder, I figured she wasn't putting me on so we were going to the closet. I wondered what her bedroom looked like. I wondered what other clothes were in her closet and how long she kept them. I thought I had a pretty good idea of her taste in clothing and was mentally creating her wardrobe. It was a fun game and I wanted to see how close my imagination was to what kinds of clothes she had when I got a look around the closet. She wore lots of pinks and purples, and I imagined a lot of loose, flowing tops and leggings.

I was so deep in thought that it was a moment before I realized that we were stationary, coming to a stop once again on the sofa. There in front of me was a needle, thread and 16 silver, shiny, shrill-sounding domes of spray-painted tin.

I had a pretty good idea from the get-go that the bells were meant for me. There was no place where they would look good;

90

maybe two or three on my tree … or just lying on the floor under the tree? There was no good place to put them, and there was certainly no good place to put 16 of them!

Okay, in her defense, she only used 14. I hope there is a way to detect sarcasm in writing, because that was meant to be very, very sarcastic. She used 14 stinkin' bells. She sewed them on my hem; yes, on the hem where she already had gold garland. Every time she picked up a bell from the table, that high-toned ring sent a chill down my spine.

You may not think it's all that bad, but I now have 14 loud, obnoxious silver bells attached to the bottom of me. You do realize that since they are on the bottom, they jingle every time Katie walks or moves, right? She was showing off her handiwork to Ron, shaking her hips back and forth, trying to trigger the tinkling sound. He thought it was cute. He has to, he married her. I, however, do not think it is cute at all!

I couldn't wait to write to you, my diary, because I knew you would agree that this was a bit over the top. And this was just the beginning. That is when it started getting really weird. Okay, weirder.

I was left on the sofa for the day. I liked it here because I could see all the comings and goings in the neighborhood. The sun shone through the big window. I could see birds, squirrels, and butterflies. I watched people as they walked their dogs, came out to put papers in the box at the end of the driveway, and got in their cars and drove off (and later came home with bags to bring inside their houses). It had been a nice day, and I was starting to feel okay about the bells. I could smell dinner starting to cook in the kitchen.

After a few minutes, Katie came into the room and turned on the TV.

"Can you please bring me the hot tea I left in there, and the Santa head that's on the kitchen table?" she called out. She then quietly started laughing as if it was an inside joke.

Ron walked in and placed a mug of tea in front of her. Holding up the Santa head, he looked at it, then turned his attention back to Katie. He turned once more and looked quizzically at the six-inch Santa head. Finally, turning silently toward Katie, Ron's expression demanded an explanation as he handed her the bearded head with the red cap.

Good. I wanted an explanation, too. Although it didn't occur to me that it had anything to do with me, there was an uneasiness creeping through every yarn of my being.

"Thank you," she smiled, barely able to keep from laughing. "That is going right here."

Then she put the creepy Santa head on my shoulder.

Oh no, no, no, she didn't!

There was no way that was going to happen to me! What was she thinking? Was this lady insane? My mind was reeling with confusion over this unexpected new turn of events. I tried to call on my higher self, but that person was nowhere to be found.

What was this girl trying to do to me? I was mortified as she sewed "creepy Santa" to my shoulder. Is it possible that she just has really bad taste? Why didn't Ron tell her? He just shook his head, and turned and walked away at her declaration that she was going to have the best sweater at the Christmas Eve party. Maybe he has bad taste, too? She seemed so happy with creepy, floating Santa on my shoulder. I really don't get it. Was it possible that she really thought this looked good?

So now that I have told you all about my day, you tell me, diary ... am I overreacting? Because this creepy, floating Santa thing has me a little freaked out.

Tuesday, December 17
Dear Diary,

I need your help. I am in fear for my life. I know this sounds a bit dramatic, but once you hear what went down today you'll be worried about me, too! You won't believe the day I had, but everything I am about to tell you is completely true.

When I woke up this morning, the first thing I saw was creepy, floating Santa staring down at me. Not the best way to start the day!

Thoughts about why he was there, how he was attached permanently, and my insane forever person flooded my mind. I was trying to process what happened when I heard him speak.

"It's about time you woke up, sleepyhead," he said in a pleasant enough tone.

But that pleasant tone didn't keep me from getting even more creeped out. All I could think was, *oh great, he talks*! For the love of God and all things holy, I prayed he was a quiet Santa. I had enough voices in my own head, and I certainly didn't need one on my shoulder that I would not be able to quiet when I needed peace. At least Katie taught me the importance of meditation … probably because she knew I would need it after she put a creepy, floating, talking Santa on my shoulder.

"I'm kinda healing from all the makeovers I'm going through," I answered shortly.

Mercifully, he took the hint and remained silent.

After a while, I started to feel bad about how I had treated him. I put myself in his shoes and realized he didn't ask to be attached to the shoulder of a sullen, pouty, and judgmental sweater. He probably expected to be on a wreath or a stocking, and instead he got me. Here I was judging him and calling him creepy, when I was the one who was not behaving well.

"It's just been a rollercoaster ride since I can remember," I said, as if that was an explanation and a conversation starter all in one. "Just when I think I am perfect, she decides that I need to have more ornaments or bells. I just want to be appreciated for who I am, or at the very least, be given a chance for me to appreciate who I am."

"Would you like me to just listen or would you like some feedback?"

I loved that question, and I took a moment to consider the answer. Was I just venting, only needing an ear to listen to me, or did I want advice? Could he possibly understand what I was going through and have any good advice, or was this something I had to sort out by myself?

Before I could decide, the door opened and Katie tossed me over her arm after greeting me with a cheerful good morning. Was she going to wear me today? Did I want to be seen with the Santa on my shoulder? I guess he was alright, but I wasn't feeling like the most attractive sweater in the closet (not that I have actually seen the closet yet).

I did not get lost in thoughts of the closet and her wardrobe, so I was completely aware when she dropped down on the familiar sofa in front of the familiar window. I did my best to keep my thoughts positive. *Happy thoughts, happy thoughts, higher self, breathe. Everything will be okay, Sophie. We are just going to hang out.* I repeated these things over and over, hoping they were true.

When Ron came in and sat next to her, I started feeling a little more relaxed. He was working from home today, doing bookkeeping work for his company.

"Okay, hold her up," he said.

Katie held me up for a couple seconds, after which she placed me flat on the vertical cushion on the sofa that usually supports a person's back. This allowed them both to see me. Ron began talking about the size of a mini fog machine, and how much work it would take to sew a fireplace on the front of the sweater. There was talk about how they could put lights behind cellophane paper in red, orange and yellow colors so it would look like a fire.

I couldn't believe what I was hearing. It was all too unreal! They were talking about adding smoke and fire to me! *They were hatching a plot to kill* me! I didn't understand any of this.

"Come look at what I found online," Ron said to Katie, and she jumped up and followed him to his office.

I started hyperventilating, "*Fire, smoke, fire, smoke, fire, smoke* …" I kept repeating these two words until I had to stop because I was getting light-headed. Just before passing out, the sound of someone else's voice startled me.

"It hasn't happened yet."

"What?" I snapped at Santa. I had forgotten all about him.

"Are you upset because you are thinking about them adding smoke to you? Why get so worked up over something that might or might not happen in the future?" he asked.

"They're trying to kill me. Don't you see why I'm upset?" I hissed at him.

"Do you want to be upset?" he pressed.

"No, that's stupid," I snapped.

He chuckled a little and said, "Okay, that's good. Then answer one question for me with a yes or a no, agreed?"

He got me. I had to agree or it would look like I wanted to be angry. Though I deserved to be mad, I didn't really want to be; so I agreed.

"Do you really think your person wants to kill you?"

Deep down, I knew she didn't want me dead. There was this contest coming up, after all.

"No, but she has no regard for my safety!" I countered, not ready to let go.

"If you are not safe, then she will not be safe. What are you *really* upset about?" Santa softly queried.

"Well, how safe is it to have smoke and fire on a flammable knit sweater? You do know I'm flammable, don't you?" I reasoned. How could he argue with that?

"Do you have smoke and fire on you now?" was the simple

question.

"No," I replied weakly.

"Chances are good that there will not be a safe way to install smoke or fire. Chances are even better that there is not enough time before Christmas Eve to get what they may need. So chances are this will never happen. So why worry about something that will probably never happen? Why not enjoy your life and think about all the stuff that makes you feel good?"

He was right. I didn't say anything for several minutes as I let go of the thoughts of imminent danger. I was not convinced that my people were being as careful with my well-being as they should be, but I decided I was probably safe for now.

That's when I came to fully accept Santa. There was no more creepy, floating, talking Santa; there was just Santa, my friend. What he said made so much sense, and he was able to make me see reason when I was too emotional to see it myself. It really made no sense at all to worry about things that may or may not happen in the future. I was going to go back to just enjoying what was going on around me now.

Then I said something I never thought I would say.

"Thank you, Santa."

Katie came back in the room and sat down to begin her daily round of renovations. Although I felt we were quite done, I didn't even care when she started sewing thin purple ribbons on the sleeve that wasn't adorned with the lights. She sewed 13 ribbons in all, in various locations all over the sleeve. I thought it looked stupid, but at this point … *whatever*. At least I was not in fear for my life.

Later, she went to the kitchen and returned with a bag of candy canes. Reaching into the bag, she grabbed a peppermint stick and, using one of the ribbons on my sleeve, secured the peppermint cane with a knot and then tied a bow to make it look good. On one hand, I had become a place to store food. On the other, it smelled really good and gave me a bit of a lift. When I smelled things I liked, such as food, candles and peppermint, it made me happy. I guessed everyone could use certain aromas to get in a better mood, too. I wondered how many others use aromas to make themselves feel good.

I was trying hard to be flexible and go with the flow. Today wasn't so bad and she probably won't accidentally set me on fire.

What do you think, diary? Now that I have told you all that has happened today, should I be in fear for my life?

Wednesday, December 18
Dear Diary,

Well, not worrying about the going up in smoke thing was short-lived. But it all worked out in the end.

It was a calm, relaxing day until just before dinner. Santa and I were still in the craft room, waiting to find out if Katie was going to test the flammability of my fibers. Santa and I had several nice conversations. It seemed he had been created long before me. He was made last season, and had spent almost a month at the bottom of the clearance bin last year before being stored until this season.

All clearance inventory stored from the year before went on a major clearance sale at the beginning of the season rather than waiting until after the holidays – to make sure the items were sold. When Katie selected the Santa from the store, she looked at him and said, "Everyone loves Santa. You will be perfect for my sweater." He was happy to have found a home and grateful to be here.

I felt better knowing that the addition of Santa was meant to enhance me and cause others to like me, not scare them away – though I still wasn't sure which effect it would have. Either way, I didn't care. Santa had become my friend, and I had become very glad he was here.

The sun was beginning to set, and the light in the craft room was getting weak when I heard Ron come home. He called out to his wife with palpable excitement in his voice. It was only a few minutes later when she came bursting into the room, grabbed me, and ran out to the kitchen.

Ron was at the table waiting, opening a couple packages lying next to a big plastic bag that said "Thank You" on it. Katie dropped me on the table and walked toward a speaker near the counter. She plugged in her cell phone, and soon they were cooking up plans while grooving to an eclectic variety of music. It seemed like there was everything from Frank Sinatra to the Arctic Monkeys. It was nice hearing something other than Christmas music, or that other music where the singers sounded so angry.

I was trying to focus on the music when they spread me across the kitchen table, looking at possibilities. They cut a piece of fabric that almost looked as if it had bricks on it, and placed it down onto the left side of my tree. After much discussion, it was decided that if "this" worked, the piece of fabric could be sewn on the front of me, on the left side of the tree. Once that was completed, it would be topped with glitter for a sparkly finish. I was starting to feel a little ill again.

"Where would we hook up the mini fog machine?" Katie asked.

"I was thinking you could sew a pouch on the back of the sweater and poke a small hole a little higher than the top of the fireplace. That way the smoke will come through," Ron explained.

"Well, if it comes out here," Katie countered, "the smoke will go right in my face. That won't work. And shouldn't the smoke come out of the chimney on the rooftop, not the fireplace?"

102

"Maybe, but smoke is cool."

There was a lot more talk about ways to push, prod and manipulate my threads so I would be equipped with special effects. They tried to find ways to incorporate fire, smoke, music and more lights. They even discussed creating a spot on the inside of my front where they could put a popper to simulate fireworks. By reaching under the sweater and pulling the string, glitter would shoot out the opening they planned to create on the front of me. Since the poppers could be replaced once they were used, she could be a walking fireworks stand. At least there were no fuses to light in that scenario.

It turned out that Santa was right. I did not have to worry about smoke and fire as there was no practical, safe way to make that happen. As a matter of fact, they set aside any talk of special effects for now and went out for ice cream. Katie put me on, and I was excited about getting out and enjoying the Christmas spirit. It was a magical time of year.

After the ice cream, we walked along the sidewalk, looking into the windows and admiring the pretty displays designed to extract as many Christmas dollars from the pockets of shoppers as possible. We came across a beautiful courtyard, and in the middle there was a breathtaking display of rose bushes surrounding a majestic fountain. There were seven students from a local high school band seated on the edge of the fountain. Each band member had a large brass instrument. There was a tuba, two trumpets, two flutes, a clarinet and an oboe. They were performing Christmas classics and doing them quite well, as those passing by paused to listen, then deposited change and dollar bills in the large jar marked "TIPS" on the front.

We stopped into one clothing store, where Katie ran into a woman she seemed to have known for a long time. After they exchanged pleasantries, both the friend and the store clerk started admiring me, saying they had never seen anything like me before. I had been concerned that my person had gone over the line, but everyone was impressed. Maybe I did have a chance in the Christmas Sweater Contest after all!

While shopping, Katie found a scarf she liked. With her mood elevated at the thought of wearing the scarf that was about to become hers, she slid into line to pay the cashier. Hanging on the checkout line "impulse counter" was a large, purple, glittery bird with a tail feather about seven inches long. I heard her squeal with delight as she declared it to be perfect. There was a clip on it, so it would stay in her hair, but I didn't think it was going to look all that great. It was too big, too ostentatious. Oh well, as long as she didn't wear it when she was wearing me! LOL

All in all, it has been a good day.

Thursday, December 19
Dear Diary,

That's it. I've had it! The lady who bought me is out of control.
The woman is certifiable and needs to be locked up. First the
lights, then the garland, next came the ornaments and the
presents. I was good with all that.

But nooooo, that wasn't enough. She tried to wire me up to have
flames coming out of a fireplace. I have shrill, annoying bells
fastened along the bottom of my hem, candy canes on my
sleeves and a bow. And I admit he ended up being cool but...
she put a six-inch Santa head on my right shoulder.

But there was still a bare spot on my left shoulder, so of course I
needed a large, purple glittery bird with a seven-inch tail! I
couldn't believe it, but that's what she did!

I freaked out when she bought the bird, and that was when I just
thought she was going to put that feathered creature in her hair
while wearing me. But then I found out this lunatic actually
decided to put the bird *directly on me*. To make matters worse,
she even sewed a three-inch stuffed elf on me, too. She bent its
long legs so it looked like he was sitting down and opening gifts
under my tree.

And she wasn't done yet. Oh no, there was more. There was also
the addition of a three-inch raccoon with big eyes. His eyes were
so big they took up all of his face, which is cute ... but I wasn't
in the mood to think about that because I was really angry, and I

had every right to be ticked off! What did a raccoon have to do with Christmas? And that was no partridge in a flipping pear tree on my left shoulder, either. She was a peacock, for heaven's sake!

There were so many emotions running around inside of me, just as so many thoughts were spinning out of control in my head. What had she been thinking? Why wouldn't she stop? I thought the idea was to dress me up to make me look good. Why would she want me to look bad when she was going to wear me to a party and enter me in a contest?

As we sat on the couch that evening, Katie making even more additions to my overcrowded front, I went from mad to deflated. It took a lot of energy to stay mad, and I was just tired. I was too numb to even think or object when the needle came around again, this time the thread attaching an angel at the top of my tree. I felt like Tall and Lanky's rooftop – a real eyesore.

Katie placed me back in the craft room, and all I wanted to do was sleep. It had been a long, exhausting day, and the only thing I knew for sure was that having new things attached to you on a daily basis for almost a week was not easy at all.

I took a deep breath, let it all out at once and closed my eyes. But I guess I was the only one who wanted to get some rest.

The elf started in. "Where are we? How long have you been here? Is it nice here? Oh, by the way, my name is Elliot. What are your names?"

I guess everyone was waiting for me to go first since, as the sweater, I was the host. But I just wasn't feeling it, and I felt way too drained to utter a single word. A big part of me wanted to reach out to the elf. Although he had been brave enough to speak first, you could hear a mild trembling and a sort of shyness to his voice. But all my energy had been drained, and I was sure that if I spoke a single syllable, the energy it took would cause me to dissolve into nothingness.

I realized some time later that I had fallen asleep. All the anger towards my person and the fear of being laughed at had been a little confusing and simply too much for me. All else was silent, but I heard the sounds of the little elf as he was doing his best to stifle his muffled crying.

"I'm sorry Elliot. That is your name, right?"

Elliot nodded affirmatively.

"I was so overtired I just shut down," I explained. "I'm Sophie. Why don't we all get to know each other?"

It really was the last thing I felt like doing. I wanted to just pretend like I was still sleeping and think about all that had happened. I needed to figure out how to process it and what to do about it. Yet the soft muffled cries of the tiny elf tugged at my heart, and before I knew what happened, the words were out.

"That's Santa up on my right shoulder."

Then to break the elf out of whatever thoughts were making him cry I asked him, "He's pretty famous and you're an elf, so maybe you two have met?"

Everyone laughed at the joke, even if it wasn't a very good one. I was glad they all got it. I wasn't sure how "sweater humor" would translate.

We all introduced ourselves and exchanged information about

our varied backgrounds. I learned even more about Santa as he shared with the menagerie. He was the oldest and by far the wisest of us all. He was the only one who was more than one season old. I have learned so much in a month, so imagine how much he has learned in a year's time!

He said he came from the south part of our country, and they talked with a funny accent. Santa did a great impersonation of what he called a "Georgia peach" that had us all howling. I was laughing so hard I was getting stitches in my sides. He had been in the clearance racks for a month after last Christmas; that part I already knew – but I'd never heard what happened after that. He was stored in a large warehouse. The Christmas items were stored right by the break room at the warehouse, so Santa had listened to many stories told by the workers, and he had learned a lot from the television always being on.

Right before Thanksgiving, there had been a fire at the warehouse. You could hear the despair and sadness in Santa's voice as he told the story. All the Christmas, Hanukah, Valentine, Easter and St. Patrick's Day items had been saved, but the Fourth of July, Back to School, and Halloween stuff all went up in smoke. All the Thanksgiving stuff was out of storage and in stores at the time of the blaze.

Santa talked about the friendships he had made, with all of them being together for so long. Oh, and I learned something cool: Santa's real name is Stephen … Stephen Albert. The real Santa just goes by Santa or Saint Nick, but all the Santas that are ornaments are individuals who have their own names.

The elf's name is Elliot. Just Elliot; no last name. He is very shy and we had to keep asking questions to get anything out of him; that is, until I asked him to tell us about his favorite thing to do.

"I have never really considered that question," he said. Then after several long moments, "I like to write poetry."

"You write?" I asked. "Let us hear something you've written."

"Well, I have made up a couple of rhymes, but I say it is my favorite thing to do because when I took a moment to think of all the things I do like to do, I feel the happiest when I think about writing and reading poetry. When I write, it helps me clarify my thoughts and feelings. And the rhythm of a poem is so soothing. Anyway, that's why I like a line that rhymes." We all laughed as he exaggerated the words, *line that rhymes.*

"We want poetry! We want poetry!" I started the chant, but the bird, the raccoon and Stephen all joined in right away, making it clear that we would not relent until he acquiesced.

"Fine," he shouted over our boisterous chorus. He paused, partially to gather his words and partially for the dramatic effect.

"In silence we stay, for that is our way,
Not knowing the joys of being fully alive.
Torn from my home, feeling alone,
Looking for love, a place I can thrive.

In the end, it's all about friends,
Others to share our hopes and our hearts,
I think I am home, no longer alone,
Now that I have friends, no longer apart."

We were all so moved by his words that it was a full minute before anyone spoke.

Elliot was quiet, wanting to hear our approval, but he didn't need to. A tear rolled out of Santa Stephen's eye, and Hillary (that was the bird's name) let out a deep sigh. He had touched us with his words, and he could tell. He could feel our silent appreciation as we each contemplated the importance of friends.

"Thank you, Elliot," Hillary started. Then the accolades rolled in as we all verbally expressed our gratitude for our elf friend's gift with words.

Hillary is the bird who roosts on my left shoulder. She told us her nickname was Hula Hoop, but we could just call her Hula. I do love her deep, rich, beautiful shade of purple, and her tail feathers were exquisite. She talked about herself a lot. I surmised that she wasn't really street smart, but she had a heart of gold and she laughed at all of my jokes. There was something I loved about someone who found even my bad jokes to be hysterically funny. I liked her a lot, although I was going to have to find a way to get her to lose the squawk. She had this high-pitched squawk that was not easy on the ears.

Hula is a peacock who is a little self-conscious. Apparently, most peacocks are known for their bluish-green color with tail feathers that fan out to display brilliant iridescent colors. They are also known for their stunning feathers (people even use them for earrings and jewelry, which I think sounds beautiful … but it freaks Hula out a little), and hers are all one color. She also shared with us that when peacocks are born in the wild, the males are the ones with the brilliant colors – but when they are created by humans, all peacocks have the iridescent coloring that makes them so famous.

"I like purple, but with me, nobody ever knows what kind of bird I am unless I tell them … because I am so plain; all one color," she lamented.

The rest of us felt this to be silliness. She really was such a rich, vibrant purple that she was mesmerizing. The added glitter on the feathers gave her dimension, giving her a bit of "bling" without looking trashy.

I initiated an exercise where each of us took a turn telling Hula what we liked about her. You know what I loved about this? We wound up all doing the same thing. We started by telling her how we all loved her coloring, and that she really was a striking shade of violet. Santa Steve pointed out how lovely her eyes are, as well. Elliot commented on how cool her feathers were. Randy the Raccoon went on about her long, graceful neck (long enough to where I'm starting to think he's a little sweet on her).

After each of us addressed her appearance concerns, we each went into what really made her beautiful. This turned out to be a wonderful exercise! You see, although we all thought she was beautiful because of the things that made her different, what's most beautiful about her was her soul. There was an innocent quality about her, a vulnerability that was easy to respond to. You could see from the start she was fiercely loyal to her friends and, at this point, even her squawk was starting to grow on us.

When everyone finished, I pointed this out to Hula, wanting her to see that the beauty that comes from within is the only beauty that really matters.

Hula blinked back a tear, and stifled a sob or two. Drawing in her breath, she looked at us with beautiful, round purple eyes.

"Thank you so much for letting me see myself through your eyes. It has made me realize that I must see the best in myself if I am to be my best self. I love you all. I am so blessed to have you. You are my family."

We all waited in silence, letting her process all her new emotions and realizations. Then she said, "Well enough about me, let's hear about you, raccoon boy. You're a cute little fellow. What's your story?"

Now I don't know if a stuffed raccoon is supposed to be able to blush, but that boy's cheeks sure were glowing at Hula's remarks, further confirming my suspicions that he had a crush on Miss Hula.

"Well, er, uh, there's not much to say."

Seemed like the bird had his tongue ... (or isn't that supposed to be a cat?).

Hula persisted with the questions. "Can you tell us about the factory where you were made? The people there? Were only raccoons created in your factory? I'm sure you have had a very adventurous life. Don't you come from far away?"

All it took was that little bit of prompting, and Randy was off.

He had been created in a place called China. He said that it was a huge factory; so large it made the Walmart Superstore where he was purchased look like a broom closet. The people there spoke a different language, so Randy was bi-lingual. He promised to teach us Mandarin, the language spoken at his birth factory. He had taken a plane to get to the United States, and although he couldn't see anything from his box during the flight, he described the sensation of takeoff and landing in the plane as the best experience of his life. He told us he had high hopes of being a toy for a child when he got here, but now realized that with us, like Hula said, he was now part of a family. With a kid, he would be played with for a little while, but then forgotten.

"But now that we have each other, I will never be alone," he concluded.

We waited for the angel to speak, but she never did. We were not sure if she didn't want to yet, or if she was just a non-thinker. A non-thinker is a someone that was created like us, rather than being born the traditional way, but they don't think and therefore, don't talk. They spend their lives just sort of existing … always the same, lacking the ability to experience thought or emotion like us. Her face was perfectly still, so we could not tell. When we asked her if she wanted to share with us she did not answer, so we assumed she was a non-thinker.

As we all wound down with our own thoughts, getting ready to drift off to sleep, I was feeling pretty good. Earlier, all I wanted was to be left alone, but now I was glad that I would never be alone. It's funny how quickly things can change.

It occurred to me that once I had taken a little time for myself, to clear my mind of all the noise and negative talk going on, I was able to restore my energy level. My mental state of mind had caused me physical distress (I've heard it referred to as stress for short). So I had to quiet those thoughts to make my physical-self feel better.

Once my mind was in a better place, I was able to reach out to the others around me who needed my support. I have come to understand the importance of managing thoughts and keeping them positive if you want to see positive results in life!

With this new, better outlook, life seemed perfect once again. I had it all; friends that were really family, a great party coming up, and a fun contest, too. I wondered if the other sweaters I knew were lucky enough to have been decorated with a new family like mine. Life is very good, diary. Sweet dreams.

Friday, December 20
Dear Diary,

I've heard the saying, *the higher you climb, the further you fall*.
Yesterday … no, even this morning, I didn't have a care in the
world. I had been chosen by a forever person who is fun, kind
and gentle; somebody who I thought cared about me. I am in a
nice home and I got a glimpse of the spacious closet I will reside
in, so I am not going to be cramped in a drawer someplace. And,
after getting to know Santa Steve, Hula, Elliot and Randy, I felt
like I had a family. If you asked me even as recently as four
hours ago, I would have told you I had a perfect life – the kind
of life we always talked about one day having when we were
first created at the factory.

What I didn't realize until now is how much I missed the good
old days when I was at the factory! Those days seemed so long
ago, and it was definitely a much simpler time. Right now, I just
want to be with my sweater family, not the collection of oddities
permanently bound to me with thread and glue. I want to see
Marci and Patricia. I want to hear my sisters laugh. I want to
have fun, and Jessica and Chloe sure knew how to do that. I
missed Leila, Tonya, Richard, Tim and Tom. I wanted to be
around other Christmas sweaters and I wondered if they all
found out about the big joke, too; you know, *the one about all of
us "ugly" sweaters being a big joke*. I don't think my sisters,
brothers and friends are ugly at all, but the rest of the world
apparently believes this to be the case.

I've never felt so alone. Not in the dark boxes being shipped to the photo shoot, at Warehouse City or at the Superstore. Not even when I woke up that one night by myself in the craft room (I was by myself until *she* added Santa, then the bird, the elf and the animal.)

I've also never felt so humiliated. The shame seems overwhelming. All I want right now is to shrivel up and die. I know that may sound like a very melodramatic statement, and it may seem I am prone to drama, but I know you'll understand once you hear what is happening.

You, diary, are my only friend. You have been here with me since I left the factory. You have listened to all the ups and downs. By writing to you, I have gained clarity, wisdom and an understanding about myself. You have allowed me to share things that I might not have otherwise looked at or explored. You've helped me make sense of things, and for that I love you and will always be grateful.

But there is no making sense of what I learned today. I do not know how to process this. I really do feel like the world has ended … at least, *my* world has ended.

This, my closest and best friend, is what happened today.

Things started out incredibly well. The sun filtered through the plantation blinds in the craft room. This was my favorite time of day. When the light came through the slats, it hit the shelves on the opposite wall where the glitters were stored. It cast brilliant prisms of rainbow colors all over the walls that would shift ever so slightly as the sun inched higher in the sky. The solar-generated light show was breathtaking and I watched in silent gratitude, feeling whole, complete and happy. It was like a form of visual meditation that I had come to enjoy over the last couple of days.

116

The first thing I noticed this morning was how considerate my "framily" was, especially in the way they treated each other. A framily is (as defined by me) the group of friends who are so close to you that they become your chosen family. Friends + family = framily.

They all awoke, one by one. First, Santa Steve re-animated. I heard a quiet yawn and noticed him look at the others. When he saw they were still sleeping, he just gave me a wink. He really is thoughtful.

Elliot's eyes popped open soon after Santa's. I used my sleeve to wave, and he nodded his understanding and returned my salutation with a warm smile.

I thought the peace and tranquility might be all over when Hula woke up. I'm not implying she isn't considerate, but she is so bubbly that, well, I guess the best way to explain it is that she just overflows sometimes. When she does, it comes out in the form of that squawk that I have come to love and find pretty darn funny. Once again she proved to be predictably unpredictable. When she woke, she simply fluttered her long, beautiful lashes, pulled her feathers around to cover her beak, hiding a nice, deep yawn. Then she smiled and rested her head against me, returning her tail feathers to their original position.

The raccoon was the last to rise, and it was a good thing. It really was funny to watch. His furry little body was lying there, still as a stone. Out of nowhere, he jumped to life, kicking and swinging, making an unintelligible grumbling noise. He then stopped, looked around with a dazed look on his face and, realizing where me was he said, "Yeah, can we not talk about that right now?" and turned a bright, fire engine red.

We all burst out in laughter, then said our good mornings to each other. I felt like the leader (or really, more like the mother) of the group because everyone was attached to me. I was the common thread … if you will forgive the pun. It was really nice, and I was feeling like I had it all, as we shared the dreams we dared to envision during our short lives.

Santa had always dreamed that he would get to meet the real Santa Claus. He could picture the scene clearly. A little child would send a note to the North Pole, asking for a Santa head for Christmas, so she could play with him and use him to decorate her room. The real Santa would select Santa Steve for this little girl or boy. The elves would make sure he was wrapped with a beautiful red bow, and he'd be added to the bag that went into the sleigh. Next, he would be taken on Santa's sleigh and meet all the reindeer, before finally being delivered to his new home.

When Santa Steve spoke of this happening in his life, his eyes moistened with tears, and you could hear the passion in his voice. He always thought this to be his destiny. But he also felt grateful for what he now had … a home and a family.

Randy just wanted to be a kid's toy, and perhaps even have a kid to play with. He also wanted to be able to stay truer to his nature. I did not realize that raccoons typically slept all day and stayed awake at night. In China, Randy told us, they had a saying: *yǒushí nǐ bùdé bù zǒu xiāngchǔ*; or in English, *sometimes you have to go along to get along.*

He was told kids would want to play all day and sleep all night. This was something he would have to get used to, even though that wasn't in his nature. In his perfect world, he would play with his forever child all night long, they would sleep all day, and his child would always let him sleep in the bed with him. That was Randy's perfect world. Like Santa Steve, Randy also felt that even if he had not hit his big dream, he had done quite well with all of us.

Elliot was an elf; that's all he ever wanted to be. He said that, while he loved poetry, he was created to make toys. He wanted to enjoy being a boy elf who played with toys and learned how they were made. Then he wanted to grow into an adult elf who worked for Santa in the North Pole. His request seemed simple enough; he just wanted to be who he was.

The bird was a different story. When it was her turn, she transformed into a glowing, radiant being, telling us how she wanted to travel to lands near and far, and experience many adventures. She realized that peacocks can only fly short distances, so she thought if her forever person crafted her into a pin and wore her all the time, all her dreams would come true. With the right forever person, she could see China, where Randy came from. They would travel to Europe and see Paris and Venice. Maybe they would even get to Moscow. And all the places in the United States she wanted to see; New York, California, Colorado … she went on and on. I was amazed at how much the bird knew about foreign countries, as well as U.S. geography and culture. We were all spellbound by the stories of where she would go and what she would do.

That's when the door abruptly opened.

Katie entered the room and snatched me up, saying something about it being picture time. She was putting me on while walking down the hall, and she almost ran into one of the walls. Once in the front room, she pulled my hem down so I wouldn't be wrinkled up. She fixed her hair, combing her fingers through it, so that any part sticking out was smoothed into the flow of locks cascading onto her shoulders.

Ron came into the room with camera in hand, asking if she was ready. She raised the first finger of her left hand in front of her as she applied lipstick with her right hand.

"Okay, let's get a couple of pictures before we head out."

Ron started pressing the button on the top right side of the camera, and you could hear the quiet swish of the shutter as it quickly opened then closed back up … letting in just enough light to capture the intended image. While it wasn't as fancy as the photo shoot I did as a model, it was still fun … although a bit rushed.

After Ron snapped a couple dozen shots, he and Katie went in the kitchen, where Katie promptly peeled me off. Ron placed the camera on the counter, and they both made a quick exit to do some last-minute Christmas shopping … at least, that's what I thought I heard as they were running out the door.

"Alone at last," I joked as we relaxed on the kitchen table next to cups from the morning coffee, and sections of the newspaper which were strewn about. Everyone laughed but Santa Steve. Although he didn't say a word, you could feel his whole demeanor was quite somber.

The others had never had that amount of attention paid to them. Randy told us he hoped the picture "went viral". This, of course, created a lot of questions as to why that was a good thing until he explained social media to us. If they posted all those pictures on their social media outlets, maybe we would be the next cool thing, he told us. I assured him we *were* the next cool thing whether we went viral or not … and we all agreed, laughing and feeling good about ourselves.

As the excitement dissipated and the conversation died down, I noticed that Santa Steve was exceptionally withdrawn. I wanted to pull him aside to talk, but that wasn't possible since we were all bound together as one.

"What's up witch you?" I asked in a feigned accent I learned by listening to one of the kids when I was in the Superstore, waiting to be selected by my forever person. But even my playful tone didn't seem to snap him out of it.

"Oh nothing at all," he said very unconvincingly. "Since this is everyone's first Christmas, let me tell you what I have heard about the way people in this area celebrate the day."

There was a forced cheerfulness in his voice that wasn't fooling me at all. I noticed it in his tone as he told us about traditions of people getting together in large gatherings and eating what would be a feast for kings. He talked about big turkeys, large hams, and meat-free options like eggplant, lasagna and other gourmet dishes. He was really embellishing all this talk about food, which was strange since we don't eat. I thought perhaps he knew we would enjoy the smells as the food was being prepared and served, but I also was perceptive enough to notice his eyes darting side to side several times. It was clear that he was distracted.

I strained to see what had him so concerned. When Santa Steve realized I was looking that way, he made a grandiose clearing of his throat before going on a little louder this time, changing the subject to gift giving.

This didn't stop me; in fact, it actually made me even more intent on uncovering what he was attempting to hide. I rolled a little to the right, and all I could see was an advertisement section from today's newspaper. I wondered if this was what had Santa Steve so agitated.

Looking closer at the ad, I saw all kinds of Christmas

decorations and toys, and … oh, OMGosh … there I was! It was one of the pictures they took when we went for the big photo shoot. I had made it big-time. I was, as Randy called it, viral!

I couldn't contain myself, and I interrupted Santa Steve.

"Hey, look! There I am. Remember how I told you I was in a photo shoot and they picked me from all the sweaters to be a model? Well that's what I looked like before we became a family! Isn't that cool? What a great honor to be …"

My voice trailed off, or I think it did as I read the print next to my picture. Santa Steve was saying something I neither heard nor acknowledged. There was a faint murmur in the background as everyone started asking questions that I couldn't hear. There it was, in big, bold letters.

UGLY SWEATER SALE

For a while, I was confused and didn't understand. It seemed like forever, but soon it all came together. *I am an ugly sweater.* I was bought from the store not because my forever person fell in love with me, but because she thought I was the ugliest sweater in the store (or she could make me ugly enough to win the contest).

The thoughts were swirling through my mind. *People think I am ugly. I am not loved. I am not worthy. I feel embarrassed, humiliated and ashamed of what I am. I am a joke.*

I turned to look past the advertisement, and my focus was drawn to a cartoon picture of another "Christmas sweater". It was an invitation to this big party I had been hearing about. Wear the ugliest sweater and win $100, it enticingly said.

I felt like my world was crashing down around me. Here I thought I was pretty flipping awesome and beautiful, only to learn that I am considered *so* repulsive they want to take pictures of me and put the word "ugly" next to my name.

So now, when I tell you my world has ended, I know you understand. Knowing I was created for the purpose of leading a life of humiliation and unworthiness, well, that is no life at all. I wish this pit of despair would just swallow me up.

I am overwhelmed right now, and I have no idea what to do or where to go. Oh, that's right … I'm just a sweater, and an ugly one at that. I can't "do" anything. I can't "go" anywhere. I'm trapped.

The scope of the situation hit me. I am going to be worn to a party to be ridiculed so my forever person, the one who is supposed to be my very best friend, can get an extra $100. I couldn't go to that party. I couldn't stand knowing she feels that way about me. I couldn't imagine a life lived in shame and humility.

No. No. No!

Saturday, December 21
Dear Diary,

I woke with the feeling that everything was wrong. There was a
knot in the pit of my Christmas tree and a lingering memory
trying its best to come back. So far, though, all I had was that
feeling of dread you get just before the memories come rushing
in and everything hits you.

Then it all did come back, in a flood of memories, feelings,
realizations and emotions. Life would never be the same again. I
had been living in a fantasy world where life was great, I was
happy, and all my dreams had come true – but none of it was
real. None of it was true. Instead, it was all a false reality I had
created for myself.

The truth was that I had been designed and created specifically
to be ugly.

The truth was I had been bought because I was considered the
ugliest of the ugly.

The truth was that my purpose in life was to be paraded around
in front of a group of people at a party and judged to see if I was
ugly enough to be considered a winner.

The truth was very painful.

I thought back to when I was first bought, and how naïve I was. I thought it was wonderful that I was selected despite my missing pom. No wonder it didn't matter! *The more damaged, the better* must have been her motto. I bet she got a big laugh when she looked at me, thinking how hideous I was, and how perfect I was for her purposes. When she said I was perfect, she meant perfectly hideous!

Then she added the garland and the ornaments, presents and lights. I thought it was so cool that I was getting a make-over, and I felt so beautiful. What an idiot I have been! And now, just when I thought it couldn't get any worse, I realized something else; I am equally as stupid as I am ugly! I had a gut feeling that something was up when she turned me into a freak show by attaching people and animals to me for all to see, but I ignored it.

Through the clouds of my pain, I heard the others talking softly to me, politely asking if I was going to be all right. We were still on the kitchen table, in plain sight of the advertisement and invitation. The mere sight of these printed pieces of paper made me want to throw up, as I alternated between feeling nothing and being completely numb, and feeling an overwhelming pain. Several times, I broke out sobbing so badly that I cried myself to sleep. It was a welcome relief to the confusion raging inside my mind.

The last time I woke up, I was in the bedroom on top of a pile of clothes. I could hear the sounds of cleaning going on outside the room, and they were moving closer. The noise of the vacuum cleaner purring from the other side of the door was calming and soothing.

I had to stop these thoughts. Ever since I saw that ad and the invitation, my thoughts had been spinning out of control, and as a result I was spinning out of control, too. I was starting to see a direct relationship between the thoughts in my mind and how I was feeling. The darker my thoughts, the worse I felt. But how could I just ignore the fact that my life was a joke? I was the joke. Only I was not laughing.

I kept my eyes closed, shutting out all the others. They couldn't possibly understand. They had been created to bring joy to people. They had real lives.

Santa Steve could spread Christmas cheer just by being himself. People would look at his face and be reminded of the spirit of giving. His rosy cheeks and bright eyes could bring a smile to even the most sullen face. He was wise beyond his years (year, actually) … and he had one simple wish – to meet the original Santa Claus. He knew he had a gift to make people happy and was pleased with his life. He even seemed to accept that he may never have his dream come true, displaying unbelievable contentment despite being relegated to playing the part of accessory on a closet-bound ugly sweater.

Randy was adorable and playful. He had extra big eyes that made him so cute. He could bring joy to any child, young or old, who liked warm, fuzzy, adorable little fur balls. I could clearly picture an equally cute little boy or girl getting hours of pleasure playing with Randy – and I imagined how happy he would be. He said he was happy playing with us, but I could still see the longing in his eyes to be held and cuddled.

I could relate. I wanted my family right now. But I knew that was another useless, hopeless wish in a useless, hopeless attempt to make me feel better about my useless, hopeless life.

Elliot. Well, Elliot was an elf … and everyone loves elves! His purpose in life was huge. He could be part of a team that created toys for children. I could think of no better purpose in life than to bring happiness to boys and girls. Even as a tree ornament or part of a centerpiece, he was a reminder of the Christmas spirit, like Santa Steve. He was cute, likeable and endearing. He had value; great value, indeed!

Hula was that brilliant color of purple and had such elegant features. She was a beauty through and through, and she was meant to fly. Her exquisite splendor was designed for many to see and appreciate. She should see Paris, Rome, New York and Hawaii. Her destiny was to see all the wonderful places on this earth that have been created for us. Whether the sites were created naturally at the hands of God or through the creativity given to people by Him, that is what Hula was born to do. If there is one thing I am certain of, one lesson I have learned in my short life, is that if we are given a desire, we were meant to have that desire fulfilled. After all, fulfilling our desires makes us feel great … and feeling good is really what life is all about.

I thought about my framily and all they had to offer. I couldn't stop the thought of how little I had to offer in comparison. I was just an ugly sweater whose only purpose was to be ugly. I had no value, unlike my friends. There were so many ways they could make the world better, and each had their own unique qualities to offer anyone with whom they came in contact.

When I finally thought I couldn't get much lower and things couldn't get worse, it did. It got much, much worse. I was horrified when I felt the full gravity of the situation.

It was bad enough finding out that I am an abomination, and that my life is a worthless joke. But it became clear that because of me … because I was going to be in a contest and *she* decided to "ugly me up" even more, I was going to keep the ones I love from having the full, rich lives they deserved. None of them would ever live a life true to themselves. Instead, their destinies and their life purposes were altered because of me.

Santa Steve would never come face to face with St. Nick. Elliot would never get to be an elf at the North Pole. Randy would never get to roam free and be true to his nocturnal nature, and Hula would be tethered to my shoulder … wings clipped, dreams crushed.

My worthless, pathetic life was all that was lying between them and the lives they were meant to live. If I didn't think I could go on one moment longer before, I was sure of it then.

I'm not sure when I made the decision or if I even decided at all. It all just seemed to happen. It was like I was watching someone else control me. My mind was numb when the bedroom door opened and the vacuum cleaner pushed its way into the room.

Katlin was pushing the large cleaning device back and forth over the rug. I felt a flash of anger toward her, thinking of the humiliation I was being dealt from her hand. All she cared about was winning her stupid contest.

As she got closer, I watched her with disdain as she sucked up all the dirt and debris on the floor. It was that very moment that I realized something; I was a lot like the dirt and debris. The only difference is they got to just be sucked up and sent to "Neverland," yet my future held nothing but degradation. I didn't want my future anymore, and I *did* want my friends to have the futures they deserved. Could I be brave enough to do the right thing?

With all my might I hurled myself to the floor. The air conditioner came on just as I made my move and that little extra momentum landed me right in front of the head of the vacuum. Before anyone knew what happened, I was sucked up into the mechanical machine … and into the sweet release of nothingness. I felt a sense of relief as the pain dissipated and the blackness offered its reprieve from the agony.

PART II

And I feel fine …
(Not Dead Yet)

Now that you know my story, I hope you will not judge me so harshly.

I know now that what I did was not smart at all, and I'm not proud of it. Even at this moment, I still think my reasons for doing what I did are valid. However, just because I think I had a valid reason, there is no excuse for my actions.

I am tattered and torn, knowing that no needle will ever make me right again … and yet, I do not care. Although what I did was not right, I still see no options for my future (at least, not any good ones). Yet I ask for your compassion and empathy as I continue to entrust you with the details of my life.

I know not where life will take me, but I will always have you, diary, my constant and faithful friend.

Sunday, December 22
Dear Diary,

When I gained consciousness it took me a minute to remember what happened, figure out where I was, and conclude that I wasn't dead. I looked around to assess the damage to the others before I looked at myself. Hula was hanging by a thread and was almost free. She looked as beautiful as ever and for the first time, I fully understood that I could have hurt the others very badly by my actions. I was so busy trying to relieve my own pain, I had not considered how my own actions can easily cause additional pain to those who are part of my life. I convinced myself that I was doing it for *them*, when in reality I was just being selfish because I did not want to face a meaningless life of people calling me ugly.

It seemed like I couldn't get anything right, but now was not the time for thinking about me. Now I had to check on the others.

"Hula, are you alright?" I meekly asked.

"Right as rain, sugar."

I started to sob.

She had every right to be angry with me, but instead showed me compassion and caring. It made me feel better and worse at the same time.

"There, there," she went on, "don't you worry about me now, I'm fine. Not a scratch."

I couldn't look at her directly. It was all so embarrassing … and confusing … and painful.

"How about you, Santa Steve?" I queried.

"That was quite an adventure, but I am unscathed. You may want to talk to Randy."

My eyes quickly went to Randy, and I could see he got the worst of it. There was a tear on his stomach, and his fluffy white guts were coming out his side. My heart sank as I examined the damage.

Before I could say a word, he cheerfully offered, "It doesn't hurt a bit. Actually, it makes me look kind of scrappy and tough, doesn't it?"

Once again the floodgates opened as I felt the love and kindness that infused his words.

Elliot was fine, for which I am grateful. I lost several ornaments and a couple gifts. The lights were okay, but two of the bells along the bottom of me were mangled.

There were so many emotions I still had to process. Yesterday, I was so overwhelmed that I shut down and somehow decided that the only solution was to end it all. Now I know I hurt those I love; if not physically, then without question emotionally. All I had been thinking about was my own situation and how much pain I was enduring. I even found a way to convince myself that my selfishness was in their best interest. But while I was processing so many things, part of me had an "aha" moment, albeit a brief one.

Yesterday, I believed that everyone's lives would be better without me. That belief was created because I kept repeating it in my mind … over and over again until I finally convinced myself it was true. The thought flashed through my mind that if I think positive things over and over, I may be able to create *a good belief system* that would make me feel better. But that thought passed quickly as I turned my attention back to my friends.

"I don't even know where to begin," I started. "I saw the ad with my picture announcing that I was an ugly sweater. Then I saw the invitation that confirmed that I am nothing more than an item of clothing designed to be frightful. It brought back memories of being called ugly at the warehouse when three girls were trying me on and taking pictures. I felt the fear of being unworthy, just like I did when the boy at the Superstore tore off my pom and tossed me in the middle of the clothes rack. I am not making excuses, but *none* of you know what it is like to be made for the sole purpose of being laughed at!"

No one said a word as I continued trying to do my best to give them the explanation they deserved.

"I could go into the fear and insecurity I felt when I lost my pom and was called damaged at the store. I would even be willing to be completely honest and tell you that when Katie first started adding all of you, I wondered why I was not enough. I would gladly explain all the reasons for feeling hopeless because of my fears, insecurity, and lack of self-worth. But all you have to do is look at me to see that the ad and the invitation were the last crushing blows. They validated everything I knew deep down about myself, but did not want to believe. That I have no value."

It was time to finally get to my point.

"I fooled myself into thinking that I was something special. But knowing that I am just a freak show and was created to be someone's joke, well, I still feel completely broken. Yet I get that it doesn't excuse how I reacted. Although my mind is still pretty twisted, I promise I will never do anything to endanger any of you again. As a matter of fact, I swear it."

"But you know, these feelings are so strong that I convinced myself that you would all be better off if I wasn't around. Hula, maybe you would be able to travel, like you always wanted. Santa Steve, maybe you and Elliot would be placed by the tree as decorations and get to meet the Big Man himself. And Randy … if you weren't tied to me, I know that any child would love to love you, and you could roam and play all night while your child slept. You are so warm and wonderful."

I was breaking up a little now, the emotions seeming to steal my words before I could say them. I took a moment, then continued.

"Fact is, I just did not want to deal with it. Mostly because I do not know how to deal with it. I did not think of how each of you could be hurt. I am so very sorry, and while I do not expect you to forgive me, I hope you know that I meant you no harm and I just … I just … I do not know what I was just doing or thinking. I am still so very confused, and now it's even worse."

After a long silence, Santa, patriarch that he was, spoke first.

"Well of course we cannot forgive you."

My eyes grew wide with sadness, then downcast in resignation of a just decision.

"There is nothing to forgive."

I looked back up at him quizzically, then to the others and back to him.

"We understand, darling," Hula chirped in. "You are not the only one who has had insecurities, or disappointments. And you are not the first to have others doing and saying things that can make you feel very small or insignificant."

I was so moved by her concern, and the looks of unconditional love in the eyes of all my friends. I was about to say something, I wasn't even sure what I was going to say … when the bedroom door opened and in *she* walked.

It was my forever person … the one I thought was going to be my best friend. *The one who betrayed me.*

She picked me up and looked me over very thoroughly. I didn't see any judgment in her eyes, but surely that's exactly what she was doing. She had been judging me since she first saw me. She judged me to be so ugly that she thought I could win her stupid contest. Somehow, knowing that I had ruined her chances of winning should have made me feel better. After all the pain she inflicted on me, I should be happy to send a little back her way. But it did not make me feel better at all; it really didn't matter.

She took a deep breath and sighed. "Well, this is going to be quite a task."

Katie tossed me over her forearm and left the bedroom. We headed through the kitchen and into the front room. We passed the hall and finally wound up in the craft room. After picking up a bag of supplies and her sewing kit, she exited there, ultimately sitting down and taking up residence back in the front room.

She just got settled in when there was a knock at the door.

"Come in," she shouted, and in walked Isabel.

"Let's have a look," Issa declared.

Great … just great. Katie called Isabel and told her I was a mangled mess. Why couldn't I just be a regular old sweater? Why couldn't they just leave me alone?

Whatever.

Isabel picked me up and looked me over. "All that work down the drain. Are you going to get a new one and start over?" she asked, handing me back to Katie.

"No! Sophie and I are in it for the long haul," Katie cheerfully said. "First, I'll pull the yarn where it is sticking out and tie it down. Then I'll darn over the hole. After that, I'll stitch up the raccoon and put him over the patchwork to hide any loose yarn. I think I'll reattach the raccoon and the bird with Velcro this time. The elf looks fine, but I'll use my paint to touch up the scratch on his cheek."

I hadn't even noticed that. I looked at Elliot, and he nodded that he was fine. My heart sank again as I thought of what I had done.

"You think you can still win?" Isabel asked her friend. "That thing is shredded."

"Of course," she replied. "My sweater is beautiful."

Wait. What?

"She is so cute to start with, then having real garland, presents and ornaments really brings her to life," Katie explained. "The lights on the sleeve are so fun, and they even blink when I push the switch all the way to the right. The bells are a little over the top, but I'm going to replace them with smaller bells that make a very soft tinkling noise which I think will be festive, but not obnoxiously loud."

She *liked* me?

"And who doesn't like Santa, elves, angels and stuffed animals?"

Isabel laughed, "Okay, what's with the bird then?"

Good question! I loved Hula, but it's not like she was a partridge in a pear tree or anything. What did she have to do with Christmas?

"The bird is my favorite color, purple, I love peacocks, and I think she is good luck!"

I thought Hula was going to lose it. It was all she could do not to fan her feathers, displaying her full brilliance in front of the two women, which we all know is forbidden. I was so happy to see how the compliments made her light up, and I was glad we would have something upbeat to talk about later.

"Okay," Isabel countered, playing devil's advocate. "You like all the decorations you have put on your sweater, but I'm sure others will be decked out, too. It is $100, after all. What is going to set you apart?"

"Our hostess Wendy said that telling the story about how we came to find the perfect sweater was part of the competition,"

Katie countered. "I've written a little story, and I was trying to figure out how to end it. Now I've come up with the perfect ending for the perfect sweater story. You see, Isabel, I don't really care if I win this contest or not. At first, that was my goal; that's why I bought her. But all the time I spent trying to decide how to dress her up and bling her out ... that was fun. Making the additions, seeing what worked and what didn't, sewing down her ornaments ... that's where the magic is, not in winning. It was great putting all this together, and just because they call it an ugly sweater contest, I still think my sweater is the most beautiful sweater ever. And win or lose, I've already won. And that is how I will end my book too."

Isabel looked quizzically at Katie, like she was missing something.

"A book?"

"Yes," Katie replied. "While the others may tell a short story about how they met their sweaters, I will be writing a short story and printing a copy for each of the guests at the party. And, I will invite everyone to take a candy cane from my sleeve. What other sweater gives away goodies? "

"And there's that," Isabel said slowly and in an exaggerated tone, a smile slowly forming on her face. Then they both broke down into a deep belly laugh.

The two of them continued talking as I processed what was happening. I had been wrong, so wrong.

Katie finished putting me back together the best she could. There was loose yarn that she creatively tucked away and hid with the extra decorations, and a hole that Randy was now covering, held steadfast with Velcro. She carried me/us back to the craft room, which looked as magical when the sun set as it did in the morning. The others stayed silent, letting me reflect on all that had transpired.

I had been happy before I knew I was an ugly sweater, when I was just a sweater. But my forever person said she did not consider me ugly, even though she was going to enter me in an ugly sweater contest.

The first thing I had to reconcile was my feelings about myself. When I thought people considered me beautiful and picked me to be a model, I was happy, because I felt beautiful and special. When I found out I was considered an ugly sweater, I felt terrible and worthless. And I was happiest when I was just a sweater.

I guess one of the things I got out of it was this: You have to be the best version of you that you can be. Then you will know that you are a person of value, with a life that has purpose. It doesn't matter what others think; it only matters what you think of yourself.

Therefore, if I really want to be happy, it really is easy. All I have to do is be me, and strive to be the best me possible.

Another lesson I learned is that you never really know what someone else is thinking. Aand even if they are thinking mean things, it doesn't matter what someone else thinks if you're doing the right thing. I guess you will never feel truly good about yourself if you allow the opinions of others to decide what you think of yourself.

Lastly, I learned that if you tell yourself something enough times, you will begin to believe it.

I was so upset, sad and crushed, that all I could think about was my poor, pitiful life. I repeated over and over again that I was bought because I was ugly, and I was nothing but a joke. I thought that my person didn't like me. I told myself that my life had no value, and that others would be better off without me. *None of this was actually true*, but I told myself these things over and over and over again ... and soon, I convinced myself it was true. I acted on that premise which was, of course, a false view of reality, colored by my pain.

Going forward, I've promised myself that I would only think and say good things about myself, and I would make those my beliefs, which would become my truths.

I knew I had to talk to everyone soon. They had been so patient with me these last two days. It seemed like I had learned so much. How could I explain all that had gone through my head, and everything I am beginning to realize?

You see, I realized that I would never be alone again. I have a family. While I am the sweater, together we are all the new version of the sweater. They are as much a part of me as the lessons I have learned.

Eventually, the time was right, and I was ready to get things out in the open. I wasn't sure what to say, and I was a little surprised by what actually came out.

"A lot has happened lately. To say I am sorry is weak and doesn't cover it," I began. "I'm not sure where all my insecurities started. Maybe it was at the warehouse, maybe at the store. But I can see where it has led me. I am so glad that each of you is all right. Yet before I tell you how this has changed me for the better and made me appreciate all of you more, I think you each deserve a chance to tell me off and express your feelings about my bad behavior."

As usual, Santa Steve started, for which I was grateful. His calm, cool and kindly demeanor was comforting at a time when I needed comfort, even though I didn't feel I deserved it.

"You don't have to tell me how sorry you are; I can see that," he rationalized. "And I don't need to tell you that your actions were wrong. Now that you are less emotional, you can see that for yourself. What you did, trying to end it all, was selfish. That is not a judgment; it is simply a fact. In life, there are people who love and need us, whether we know it or not. In the larger sense, we are all one and interdependent on each other. While that means we each have a responsibility to each other, it also means that we are never alone."

He wasn't done. After letting that thought sink in for a moment he, continued.

"What saddens me is that you were not aware that of your great value, not just because we are attached to you, but because of your soul, your essence, the energy that you carry. And for that I have to apologize to you."

Was I hearing things wrong? *Him* apologize … to *me*?

The countenance of the jolly man was quite serious as he went on. "I should have let you know how much I appreciated you," explained Santa Steve. "I should have seen that with all the changes thrown at you so fast, you may have needed a little extra reassurance. I should have been a better friend and communicated your value to you. And for that, you have my most sincere apology."

Santa stopped. My whole sweater was racked with sobs, and he was intuitive enough to know I had to process the words he had already spoken before I could take in anything else.

I had done this terrible thing to him and the rest of my friends, and here he was apologizing to me! While his words made a huge impact all by themselves, his compassion spoke volumes. The fact that he cared enough about me to want to make me feel better when he had every right to be angry, drove home all the realizations I had discovered over the last 24 hours. His wisdom and caring personality were amazing, as he put his emotions aside to help me in my moment of need.

"You aren't mad at me?" I asked.

"Child, the only time people get mad is when they take things personally," said the bearded saint. "I know this had everything to do with how you were feeling and nothing to do with me. Now, if I thought you didn't learn your lesson, I would be concerned. Instead, I am pleased that you have come to a new awareness through this, which I look forward to hearing about when you are ready to share."

"Well, I have a mouthful to say," squawked Hula. "Girlfriend, what in the world *were* you thinking? Yes, I did get my feathers ruffled a little, but why did you shut down and try to handle this all by yourself when you have a whole lot of us who love you? You are the glue that holds us all together. Without you, we wouldn't be a framily. I plan to drum that into your little brain for the rest of your life! Whatever you were thinking, stop it. I understand that sometimes life deals you some challenges, but when they seem too big or too heavy, that's when you reach out for help. Give us the joy of helping someone we love. Give us the joy of helping you!

"Let me tell you 'bout what happened when I was still in the store," she continued, barely taking a breath between sentences.

146

"I'd been carelessly tossed in a bin, my longest feather twisted to the right. It hurt quite a bit, and I was trying to get it straightened out while there were no humans in the room. But we were all squished in so tight you'd have thought we were sardines in a tin. A nice young elf, much like you, Elliot, offered to help. At first I told him to buzz off, because I could handle my own tail. But I kept struggling. Eventually, it became plain to see I could use some assistance. I told him to mind his little hands and behave, and I would *let* him help me."

"I may have been a little more 'stuck up' back then," she confided.

Hula paused only to take a quick breath, and then continued. "After he straightened out my tail, he told me how he used to help everyone at his warehouse, so he felt useless until I came along and needed help. He had actually been getting a little depressed. '*Letting*' him help me, did him as much good as it did for me.

"Just like the ocean washes ashore and then falls back to sea in a constant back-and-forth motion, so is life. Sometimes you give and sometimes you get, but you must allow both. And next time, Missy, you better allow your framily, no, your FAMILY … to help you. As long as you promise me that, we are good."

"I promise, I promise," I said – and I meant it. Not only was it a relief that she wasn't mad, the exhilaration of having such a great support team instantly lifted a giant weight off my shoulders. I felt lighter than I had since I had seen the newspaper ad and invitation.

"Well, all right then," Hula replied.

I knew that Elliot and the raccoon were younger and might be less forgiving. I had been let off easy so far.

All eyes were on Randy, and he was ready for his turn. "Don't look at me. You know what you did was dumb, but now I'm attached with Velcro. I bet if I wiggle hard enough at night, I can get loose and go exploring. I'll get to play at night since that's when the people sleep. Just keep it down in the day when I need my rest, you got me?"

We all started laughing at the much-needed comic relief. There is nothing like a good laugh to break up tension. With tears through the laughter, I was watching Elliot because he had not yet had his chance. Elliot's laugh was whole-hearted, but his body language indicated that he had not let the situation go just yet. That was okay; I deserved whatever he was going to say and I wanted to hear it.

"Elliot," I softly prompted.

He looked up at me with big tears in his eyes. "You have become like a mother to me," he half shouted. "Don't do that again!"

And then, he took his thin long arms and gathered up as much yarn from my body as he could in a tight hug. That cut deeper than anything else he could have said. To see his hurt and confusion tore my heart to pieces.

I promised him, too, and told him how very sorry I felt. He knew I meant it, but it was another five minutes before he loosened his hold.

Another important thing I learned was that everyone has people who love and need them. They may not know it and they may not believe it, but they do.

After a long silence, Santa Steve suggested we all just rest and meditate tonight, reflecting on all the lessons we had learned,

148

and the depth of our new and closer bond.

Monday, December 23
Dear Diary,

I woke refreshed, feeling good and optimistic. It was a few moments before I remembered what I had done. Hula noticed I was awake. She also noticed the smile that had been on my face when I had first stirred was fading fast.

"What is it, girlfriend?"

"Just remembering how stupid I was and what it could have cost all of you," I softly replied.

"Well, then, I guess we should run through this together. How about it?"

I wasn't sure what she was getting at, but I figured it was best to play along. I was feeling like I kind of owed everyone anyway.

"You are thinking about what you did in the past and it's making you feel like you drank pickle juice and milk, right?"

"Well, something like that," I answered. She sure had a way of painting a picture.

"Can you do anything to change what you did?" she pressed on with the questions.

"No," was my short reply.

"Do you have a lot to look forward to with the party, Christmas day and hanging out with us … hint, hint?"

I laughed at her playful tone as I responded in the affirmative.

"Does it make you happy to think about some of the fun stuff we have coming up?"

Now I could see where she was going.

"Yeeessss," I said, letting her know that the answer was indeed obvious.

"Then tell me this, does it make a lick-a sense to dwell on the mistakes you have made in the past if you have indeed learned your lesson?" she asked in an exaggerated manner, already knowing what answer to expect.

I pursed my lips and brought my brows together in full thought and then slowly answered, "Well, that depends."

She looked surprised, as if there were no possibility for any other answer than no, it does not make sense.

"On what?"

"What's a lick-a sense?" I asked.

I didn't know the others were up until I heard the whole group burst out in laughter. We knew what she meant, but that thick southern drawl always caused us to have to translate her words into proper English.

What a great way to start the morning! I was feeling good again, and I realized I did not have to continue punishing myself to show them I was sorry. They knew it and really loved me. When you love someone, you don't want to see them hurt any further, even when they make a mistake. Instead, you want to see them learn and grow. I was really feeling blessed.

"You are right, Hula. If I want to lead a happy and fulfilling life and be the best friend possible to all of you, I will need to keep my thoughts on possibilities, opportunities and all the things I have to be grateful for.

"I came to understand many things yesterday," I continued. "I thought maybe I could share a few and then we could talk about ways to stay positive and upbeat when something tries to bring us down."

"I'll just remember how much fun I had last night playing in the laundry room," Randy said of his first night of independence. "Those clothes smelled so fresh and clean. I nestled in them and made little tunnels, burrowing through armholes and pant legs. That made me so happy. I have never felt so free before."

Randy was able to pull himself free from the Velcro and had been running wild all night. He was clearly tired but very excited about his first night exploring our forever home. He spent the next hour telling us all about the other rooms in the house that we had not yet seen. The masked fur ball had been spying on Ron and Katie when they got ready to go to sleep, and he shared a lot of strange things they did.

Randy described one of the silliest things done by both Katie and Ron. Just before bedtime, they entered a room that offered multiple sources of water. Each of them had thin plastic sticks with plastic hairs on them. They pulled a tube of something out of a drawer and squeezed the white stuff in the tube onto the short, thin plastic hairs. Then they would put the sticks in their mouths and move them in a brushing motion across the tops of their teeth, then the bottom of their teeth. They would finish up this ritual by spitting out what was in their mouth, taking a sip of water and swishing it in their mouth and spitting that into the sink, as well.

You should have heard Randy laughing as he told of the silly activity.

This room sounded fascinating to us, and Randy continued. There was a small enclosure inside this room with a glass wall. Randy told us that our people open the door, and when they pull a handle on the wall it starts raining in there. Then they take off all their clothes and hop in. It must be some kind of game they play, because he also said that they both put bubbles in their hair and then the rain rinses them out. And the girl, Katlin, sings when she's in there.

It was going to take a while to figure out if Randy was kidding. It would also take time to learn why our people did these odd things. I was looking forward to it.

The future looked bright. I felt good. I had the best of friends and best family anyone could ask for, and my forever person truly did love me.

After a bit, Randy started winding down. The reliving of his exploits was mixed with yawns, and his tale-telling was slowing as his eyes got heavier. Before long, he started drifting off to sleep. It was really nice to see him so happy and alive. His happiness and positive energy was contagious.

Then a thought occurred to me.

When you are happy and feeling good, it makes other people

feel good. People like feeling good … so they will like being around you. And when they are feeling good, they will make other people feel good. So being happy and feeling good is one way to change the world.

Ka-boooom. That was the sound of my mind exploding.

"Hula, what tricks do you have for us about staying positive?"

"You can always be happy when you know a little secret that I'll share with you. Pretend is your friend, girlfriend … pretend is your friend. When I want a little pick-me-up, I imagine things that make me happy. You see, once we have gone through any experience, it becomes a memory. I want to go to Spain. Once I do it, it becomes a memory. Now if I imagine going to Spain, I still am creating a memory of what I have imagined."

The wheels in my mind began to race as I listened intently.

"So I imagine going to all the places I dream of one day visiting," she continued, "and in my imagination, I can really fly – and I don't mean like other peacocks, who can only fly a few feet at a time. No, I am able to soar like an eagle! And I get the most interesting aerial views when I fly. The other birds up there are always nice, and in all my adventures I can stay safe since it's just my imagination."

Hula went on about the places she visits in her imagination. There were lands I had never heard of that she seemed to know all about. "I even have a pretend boyfriend named Rico," she laughed. "He is the perfect man. Always says the right thing, knows when to listen, and he thinks all my jokes are funny. And when he preens his feathers, I gotta tell ya, he knows how to make a sensible girl go all giddy. That's right, my sister … pretend is your friend."

Considering my state yesterday, it was a pretty good morning. I liked it when Hula referred to me as her sister. I know "girlfriend" is a big part of her vocabulary, but it somehow made me feel closer to her when she called me sister. Funny how when someone says something nice, it makes you like them more.

We all looked at Elliot as I asked, "How do you stay upbeat?"

"Well, I like to think about making toys and giving them to kids," Elliot began. "There is something about making children happy that makes me feel my life is worthwhile and has great value. Don't get me wrong; if all I ever did was make toys that would be good enough. Just knowing where they are going and what it means to the kids makes me very happy. But I have never seen a child open a gift, and I always imagine the look of surprise and delight on their little faces when they open the perfect gift. You know … the one they wanted so bad but didn't think they were going to get?"

"So, pretend is *your* friend too?" Hula asked Elliot.

"Yeah, I guess it is," he said. "And I know that somehow and some way, that will happen for me. Again, don't get me wrong. I love all of you and I love being here. I'm not alone or lonely anymore, and you have made me feel like I belong. You will always be my family, but I know that I was made to be a real elf. I was created to make toys and bring joy to children. And because I have total faith that this is my purpose in life … it *will* happen. Even though I don't know how, I am at total peace because I am certain it will. And I will just enjoy every minute I have with all of you until my destiny fulfills itself. Does that make sense to all of you?"

We were all taken aback. This boyish being was wise beyond his years. His absolute faith that the universe was conspiring to bring all his desires to him at the exact time that would benefit him most was inspiring. His quiet confidence instilled the same confidence in us, and we had no doubt that Elliot would be in our hearts forever, and in our lives for only a short time.

"That makes perfect sense, Elliot." I responded.

We all stayed in silence for another moment, letting the wisdom of Elliot's words and the full value of his message soak in.

"And I imagine sitting in the middle of the floor, covered with soft bunny rabbits of all colors," Elliot blurted out, breaking the silence and creating a wave of laughter throughout the room. I loved his contrast of being confident and secure, while still keeping all the great qualities of a young boy. It was a nice combination of wisdom and innocence.

Once the sounds of merriment subsided, you could hear us in unison.

"Santa Steve?"

"Ho, ho, ho," he chuckled, sounding exactly like the real deal. "Haven't you heard? I was born jolly." He let out a belly laugh that had us all in stitches.

"Being happy is the only thing that makes sense to me. If I worry about the mistakes I have made, well I can't change them … and it only makes me feel bad. I don't like feeling bad, so I don't. I do make sure that when I have made a mistake, I learn my lesson from it. That's why I can leave it behind. I also know that because I have learned something new, I have become a better person. And the bigger the mistake, the more important the lesson I learn; and the more I grow. So, even my mistakes should be celebrated as victories; not that I set out to make them, mind you."

"And when I do look forward to things that will come in the future, I do so trusting that all will happen just the way it should," he continued. "This way, I have no worries or fears tugging at me. Those feelings also make me feel bad ... and like I said, I don't like feeling bad, so I don't. Instead, I look to the endless possibilities of the future, and just appreciate what I have going on now. I completely relate to you, my son," he said looking at Elliot.

We all stayed silent and let them have their bonding moment. It was touching.

Next, it was my turn.

"I have learned a lot over the past few days," I shared. "While I was not able to just flip a switch to be happy when I was so upset I wasn't thinking straight, I did figure out some things. I started feeling bad when I started thinking negative thoughts. I had dark thoughts about myself, my forever person and why I was even alive. The more I got twisted in those thoughts, the worse I felt. I know I cannot just decide to be happy and instantly become happy, but I can decide what to think. When I choose my own thoughts and select the ones that make me feel good, I can go from feeling bad to feeling better ... and eventually to feeling happy. So in a way, I can choose to be happy by thinking happy thoughts. Does it feel that way for any of you?"

The conversation turned quite lively with the introduction of that question. We all agreed that learning to select our own thoughts rather than just letting whatever entered our minds bounce around all day was the key to happiness and true freedom.

With that, we all started brainstorming. That was the word they used when the janitor played the self-help audios back at the factory. "Brainstorming" is what they call it when brilliant minds get together and come up with all kinds of ideas on a subject.

Here are a few things that we knew or had heard about to make you happier. I think some of these are for people only, but one day when I am gone and everyone reads my diary, I want people to benefit from what I have gone through, as well. So here goes:

1. Each day write down three things for which you are grateful. It will trigger the feeling of gratitude, which will make you happy.
2. Write a short story about an experience you had that made you happy. Maybe it was catching a fish, or being on a vacation with family.
3. Sing a song that makes you happy. Singing releases chemicals from your brain that make you feel good.
4. Reach out to a friend. You will both feel good from the connection.
5. Smile. Just looking at yourself in a mirror and smiling for 30 seconds will get you out of a bad mood.
6. Give someone a sincere compliment. There is always something positive you can find about someone, and they will appreciate being appreciated.
7. Write a thank you note. Saying thank you is great, but when you write a note you bring a stronger energy to that gratitude. You also feel the anticipation of making someone happy as the note is sent off, and you get to feel good again when the recipient acknowledges your note. This is a great way to extend the feel-good vibes you are sending.
8. Write a note to someone you haven't seen in a long time, telling them what you appreciate about them.

9. Do something nice for a stranger you will never see again. People call this Random Acts of Kindness; we decided to call it Major Karma Score.
10. Encourage another to reach for their dreams. Sometimes, just a little water on the seed of someone's dream is all it needs to grow.
11. Listen to music. Music is a universal language that engages our souls. We have decided that few are immune to its power.
12. Meditate. This is one of the most important things you can do for your mind, body and soul.
13. Read an inspiring story of someone else's triumph and victory over adversity. It will allow you to see hope and possibility for your future, and there is something about cheering another on that makes you feel good too.
14. Donate your time to helping others. This is a Big Deal Major Karma Score. That's where the other person may seem to get something out of your actions, but the feeling you get in return is really worth a lot more than you give. Okay, now you know some of our secret phrases.
15. Leave love notes around the house for your partner, or just kind notes for a roomie.
16. Always believe something wonderful is about to happen. You will be surprised at how often little miracles do happen when you are expecting them.
17. Whistle. We heard a song called "Just Whistle While You Work," but we concluded that whistling anytime was a good thing.
18. Play with a puppy, kitten or bunny rabbit. Soft, furry things that lick your face apparently make humans happy. We aren't sure on this one, but we have all heard it so we are adding it to our list.

19. Enjoy a day in nature. The oneness and feeling of belonging to a greater whole will make you feel calm and serene (unless it's raining, then you may feel a little wet, too).
20. Look through old pictures or videos. The memories triggered will release feel-good endorphins to your brain, which will make you happier.
21. Stretch yourself physically. Moving your body keeps the flow of life going.
22. Stretch yourself mentally. Moving your mind also keeps the flow of life going.
23. Light some candles. The energy of a candle light holds a special soothing effect that will elevate your own energy.
24. Try a bubble bath. No, bubble baths aren't just for kids!
25. Treat yourself to a massage.
26. Treat yourself to a home facial. You can find many fun homemade recipes to soothe and smooth your skin on this thing called the Internet.
27. Make a list of all your good qualities. Don't be shy.
28. Make a list of people in your life you are lucky to have. Also, make a list of people lucky to have you in their lives.
29. Use aromatic oils to boost your mood. We all smelled great foods cooking in our forever home, as well as the warehouses that we came from … so we know this one is true. We also like the smell of roses, fresh rain and the candles Katlin uses. I'm sure there are more scents that we will get to explore as time goes on.
30. Enjoy a nap. We do this a lot and highly recommend it.

31. Plan a picnic or day at the beach. Changing your routine by eating someplace new can increase your sensory input and allow you to think in terms of possibilities, and that will make you happy. Plus, we heard the beach is awesome and hope to see it firsthand someday.
32. Listen to a comedian or tell a few jokes. Laughter really is the best medicine.
33. Plan something fun at least once a month. Having something to look forward to keeps you happy.
34. Learn to forgive. And that includes forgiving yourself.
35. Have a heart-to-heart with someone you like. Cultivate that friendship.
36. Avoid comparisons. We are each unique and have great value. No two snowflakes are alike, yet each is magnificent and brilliant in its own right.
37. We all agreed that people can get happier by eating foods they love. I know I got happier when I smelled foods, so I can relate to this.
38. Tell someone why you love them. People love to hear they are loved, and if you tell them why, their subconscious mind tells them they are worthy of that love. As a result, they feel even better, which makes you feel better, which makes the people around you feel better, and so on.
39. Look at something with colors you like. Watching the sunrise or sunset and seeing the prisms of color in the craft room was really cool, and made us happy, too. When we were in the craft room, there was something wondrous about the random rainbow of colors splashed against the wall, when the light filtered through the window, which gave us a sense of awe. So we decided that colors can make you happy, too.

40. Look for a child who is happy and laughing. Did you know laughing can be contagious, just like a smile? Santa Steve told us about a time when one person started laughing at a joke so hard that before long the whole room was laughing, even though most of the people in the room never even heard the joke.
41. Writing poetry. This was one of Elliot's favorites. He was very good, too.

It was a really good day. It made us happy to think of ways to be happy. I knew I would never feel isolated and alone again. I also knew just what to do when the dark thoughts started creeping in.

All at once, the door flew open and Katie grabbed me, pulling me over her head and pushing her arms through my sleeves. Randy had just only been awake a few minutes, and we were all a little confused. The party wasn't until tomorrow. Was it the night before Christmas already?

Katie stopped in the hallway, peeking into the living room.

"Are your eyes closed?" she asked the little girl in the middle of the room.

"Yes, yes, yes," joyfully shouted the child. Her soft, black hair was quite shiny. She was very small and looked to be about six years old – the same age as the girl in the wheelchair I saw at the store where I was bought. She was dressed in a pink long-sleeve top with rhinestones in the shape of a heart on the front. She had matching pants that flared out at the knee in exaggerated bell bottoms. One pant leg had the same rhinestone heart on it, as well. The child had a big pink ribbon in her hair, and everyone in my family let out a very soft sigh as we fell in love with the dark haired little angel.

"What do you think, Miya?" asked my forever person.

The little girl clapped her hands with glee as she opened her eyes. "I love her. She is beautiful. Will you make me one just like her? Please, please, please, Auntie Katie?"

Katie pulled the little girl close in a hug. "Of course I will," she promised.

Then something really cool happened. Elliot got to see his first child open a Christmas gift.

Ron left the room and came back in with a large purple box with a bright pink bow on top. These were Miya's favorite colors, and she let out a squeal of delight when she saw it.

"Is this for me?" she asked, eyes big as saucers when the colorful gift was placed before her.

"Sure is, little one," Ron replied.

Miya looked at Katie and asked, "Can I open it now?"

It looked like she was holding her breath as she waited for the answer.

"Of cour ..."

Before Katie could finish the second word, Miya let out another squeal as she nearly assaulted the package. Grabbing the bow and quickly tossing it aside, she was ready to peel off the metallic purple wrap. With the taped edge in hand, Miya pulled the paper in one long strip and was able to see part of the gift. She stopped unwrapping her gift and began jumping up and down with her arms in the air.

"Yes … yes … yes!"

She turned and ran into first Katie's arms, then Ron's, showing her appreciation with the tightest hugs she could muster.

"This is awesome!" Miya exclaimed.

Everyone in the room was smiling from ear to ear. Ron and Katie bought their niece an Easy Bake oven. They knew it was Miya's dream to become a master chef when she grew up.

I felt something wet and looked down. Elliot could not hide the tears streaming down his face as he witnessed Miya's sheer joy over the gift she had received. We were all so happy for him. Each of us felt as thrilled as we would have if one of our own dreams had come true. You know you really love someone when you are as happy about their dreams coming true as you are when your own do.

Miya was adorable. She started making little cakes, first mixing the powdered mix with water, and then pouring the batter into the tiny cake pans. While the cakes were baking, she talked Katie into going online with her so they could order one of my sisters – a smaller version of me – in a child's size small. They made plans to "bling" my sister out together.

I was glad I would be there to explain things to her when she arrived, and I was very excited that I was going to see one of my other family members soon. In that moment, I fully comprehended that my framily was as much my family as the sweaters that looked just like me. My sweater family was the family I was created into, and the people in my heart were family I had chosen. Both were very important.

165

Later that night, Katie carefully folded me and placed me in her closet. As I drifted off I thought, *how could it get any better*?

Tuesday, December 24
Dear Diary,

What a night. It was the night to end all nights!

The day started with everyone in a good mood. Everyone was looking forward to getting out and going to the party tonight and there was an excitement in the air, almost palpable enough to be cut. We were in the closet, laughing and singing Christmas songs we'd heard over and over the past couple weeks, having a good old time.

Katie came in to grab me for the party, and she looked stunning. Her long, sandy blonde hair was curled in loose, large curls that framed her round face. She had makeup on, too, and looked beautiful. I never loved her more.

It was not because she looked so good (which she did), but because I realized how true her heart was at all times. She never meant to hurt my feelings, and never had a mean bone in her body. She just wanted to have fun with a contest, and she really got into the spirit of it. If she wasn't such an overachiever, I would not have my fantastic new family. She really did love me no matter what, and knew that the time you spend with someone is more important than anything else. I can honestly say that my life is perfect at this moment.

Ron was wearing a plain green sweater. Around his neck was a piece of silver garland shimmering in the light. Attached to it –

and being supported by it – was a small TV-like device, and on its screen was had a video of a burning fireplace. They called it an iPad mini when they were pressing the buttons to make the fireplace appear. Simple, but cool!

They were ready to leave. Ron picked up a bag containing two pumpkin pies and a container of whipped cream, and another bag that held two bottles of wine … and out the door we went. My sweater family and I were all excited about getting out of the house and seeing new things.

I was also beginning to get a little nervous. Although I had no chance of winning, some of those uncomfortable old feelings about being judged started coming back. What if they saw the hole that Randy was covering? Were my ornaments on straight? Would they love my friends? Would they laugh at me?

As I became more uncomfortable, I stopped and asked myself why I was selecting these thoughts. I started to change the way I was thinking and instead began asking questions like, *What will this new house look like? What will the other sweaters look like? Will the partygoers applaud me and the creativity that went into blinging me out?*

Most of all, I was curious about the story Katie was about to tell. I'd heard her and Isabel talking about how each contestant would tell the story of how they met their sweater, and why they think their sweater should win the contest. She'd told Isabel she would not only tell her story, but she also had a book for each guest to go along with it. She had completed the book, but since she wrote it when I wasn't around, I had no idea what it said.

After traveling for what seemed like a long time, we pulled up to a house where many cars were parked outside. There were lights outlining the house, and a beautiful gold wreath with pine cones and ribbons occupied the front door. Tall candy canes lined the walkway, and the festive atmosphere could be felt before you even entered the home.

Another couple pulled up as we exited our vehicle. Katie and Ron waited for them, and there were enthusiastic hugs and greetings exchanged before they stopped to examine each other's attire.

Judy was wearing a sweater featuring kittens playing under a tree. Her boyfriend, Nate, was wearing a sweater with an elf smoking a cigar on the front. The smoking elf was a little out of character, but really, these sweaters were not ugly at all. It looked as if Judy and Nate didn't want to join in the competition. Maybe they were making a statement on behalf of sweater cruelty everywhere.

Whatever the case, I really liked the kitten sweater. One of the little balls of fur was grey. She had a quizzical expression on her face, accompanied by her little tongue sticking out. You could see the head of another black kitten poking out of a gift bag with a bow on its head. *Adorable!*

Judy and Nate howled when they got a look at me; at least, it started as a howl, and then progressed into fits of giggles as they took in the full effect of me. Maybe they were laughing about me, but I was no longer offended. I was arranged in a creative and unusual way, and it seemed to make them happy.

"This sweater is great," exclaimed Judy as she stared with an incredulous look on her face. "Where in the world did you get it … or did you make it?"

"You'll hear all about it when I tell my story," Katie answered.

Together we walked to the front door, the two couples asking about each other's lives as we progressed. The door was opened before anyone knocked and we were welcomed to the party by a big, boisterous man who went by the name of Tom and his cute wife Wendy. Tom's sweater had only a Santa suit on the front, and with Tom's head on top, it looked like he was a version of Santa with a very big head and a tiny little body. It was kind of weird, but funny. Not judging, just saying; okay? She, on the other hand, looked great in a blue sweater with snowflakes on it!

We entered the house and were met with soft, soothing music and great-smelling food. There were a couple dozen people already there. Katie weaved through the guests, stopping to catch up with her friends as she spotted them. She knew a lot of people, and we were having a blast. Ron was standing with a group of guys around the television where a football game was being played.

I had stopped being nervous ... until they announced that the contest would begin in five minutes.

When I realized I was feeling nervous, I knew it would be good for me to immediately change my outlook. I decided that I was excited instead of nervous. It felt similar, yet excited was a positive emotion. I was so excited I barely heard any of the other stories when the forever people spoke about how they had found their sweater.

Judy was next; then it would be Katie's turn. Apparently, Judy was entering the contest, and all she said was she bought her sweater because the two cats on it reminded her of her own cats, Midnight and Thunderball. Then, she showed a picture where she posed her cats to look just like the ones on her sweater. I thought that was incredibly clever, even while I was still wondering what Katie was going to say.

170

Just like that, we were next. All eyes were on us and I was feeling so "excited" I thought I would jump right out of my yarn!

Ron had distributed copies of the booklet to everyone just as Katlin began speaking.

"When I bought my sweater, I wanted the cutest ugly sweater I could find," she began. "Now I *know* that they are called ugly sweaters, but I think all things Christmas are cute, and I bought the most adorable sweater I could find." Katie held up her copy of the booklet. She opened the book to a page showing a picture of me in my original condition, when she first bought me.

"And I never wanted my sweater to feel like an ugly sweater, so I decided to dress her up." From there, she went through my entire makeover history, showing the transformation picture by picture. Then she put the pictures down and started talking from the heart.

"Originally I was decking out my sweater to win this contest. Yet as I added each unique and awesome ornament or trim, I grew to love her more. I've even named her Sophie, and I think she is the world's most beautiful sweater. You see, I almost lost Sophie; she fell to the floor and was sucked up by the vacuum cleaner. And although she is mended, it's her scars that add character to her, and they have strengthened the bond between my adorable sweater and me. I plan to wear her after Christmas, and all year long. You see, my sweater is like a longtime friend to me now. I love our history and I love her."

Katie took a sweeping bow as the crowd cheered. She was the last contestant. After she finished, the voting started, but Katie continued blowing kisses to the audience while they placed their ballots in the box.

I didn't think we had a chance, but Katie spoke so eloquently. I was feeling our bond and closeness after hearing her kind words, and I allowed myself to imagine them calling our name.

In my mind, it went something like this: The party grew quiet as Big Tom came to the center of the room. He called the third-place winner, and the audience clapped and shouted their approval. The second-place winner was announced, and I just knew my name would be next. I thought that somehow I might place and now that only the winner was left to be called, well, it just had to be me.

As Big Tom called my name of the winner … *my name*, the crowd was cheering … and I was moving to the center of the room.

Hey wait, I really was moving towards the center. And Katie had her arms up, dancing a victory dance. Had he just… he did!

"That's right, the winner is Katie, and her prize winning sweater Sophie."

They really *were* calling my name. It seemed surreal. Katie was jumping up and down, and she started doing a silly little dance. She stopped and posed for pictures as she made her way to the middle of the room to collect the grand prize. Everyone was having a great time, and today was the best day I ever had. Not just because I won, though that felt good, too!

We got home before midnight, and Katie put out a plate with two cookies and a small glass of milk. She took me off and laid me on the sofa by the Christmas tree. The tree was all lit up, splashing a brilliant purple and silver light show on the ceiling.

It was beautiful, quite a sight to behold. I fell asleep admiring it, bathing in its warm, violet glow.

LATER THAT NIGHT...

I really did not think today could have gotten any better, but it did!

Just before midnight, we all woke to sounds in the living room. At first, we were all a little dazed since we had just fallen asleep (except for Randy, who had napped most of the day). I'm sure I was not alone in thinking I was still dreaming when I saw *him*.

It was Santa Claus, Saint Nick, Kris Kringle, Father Christmas … it was *the man*! He was bigger than life, and as it began to sink in that Santa Claus was right here, in our living room, we all became instantly wide awake and mesmerized.

Elliot spoke first, "Santa, is it really you?"

Santa looked around and then noticed me and my family. "Was that you, young man?" he asked, looking directly at El.

"Yes," he whispered, now almost paralyzed by fear from the attention he was getting from his idol.

"Well, I haven't met many talking ornaments, especially ones who recognized me. You must be very special."

He addressed the group. Do all of you talk?"

Everyone spoke at once and Santa started laughing, his whole belly shaking. He slowly sat down and said, "One at a time. I've got all night."

"But Santa, what about getting all the toys to the boys and girls? Aren't you on a tight schedule?" Elliot asked with great concern.

"No, not at all," was Santa's jolly reply. "I have as much time as I decide to have. That's the secret to making time stand still. Some call it magic, but I know that when you give 100% of yourself all the time, you will never be short on time. So let's talk."

Hula asked about faraway places, and Santa relayed vivid accounts of places he'd seen. Randy asked if he was being bad by sneaking around at night, and Santa assured him that he was just being true to his nature – which was actually quite commendable. Santa Steve and Santa shared wisdom, and Elliot stayed quiet.

"You know Santa, Elliot has always wanted to go to the North Pole and make toys for the kids. You are in the business of making dreams come true, aren't you?" I asked.

Santa smiled and gave me a wink. "Well, of course I am," he chuckled. Then he turned to Elliot. "So, young man, you want to make toys at the North Pole. Is that true?"

"Ye... ye... yes Santa, more than anything. Ever since I can remember having a memory, that's all I have thought about. Before I even knew there was a place like the North Pole where all you did was make toys 364 days a year, making things for children to play with is all I've ever wanted. I was created to make toys; to know that I am making children smile."

We all started laughing. Elliot, who had been so shy, got so excited when speaking of his passion that he almost stumbled over his words.

"Well, how would your friends feel if I took you back to the North Pole with me and made you a full-fledged, toy-making elf?"

Elliot sat there, too stunned to speak. The possibility of having all his dreams come true seemed larger than life to him.

We all started talking at once, voicing the same sentiment; we would miss him very much, yet would be so very happy for him to have this opportunity to fulfill his life's purpose. What a way to roll into Christmas!

Santa gently released Elliot by cutting the threads that bound us together, and we said our tearful goodbyes. He was off to live his dream. Santa promised to bring him back for a visit every year when he came. After he left, we all were pensive, lost in thought, as we drifted back to sleep.

Wednesday, December 25
Dear Diary,

Today, Katie wore me again … not to stay warm, not to win a contest, but because she loves me.

I have to say, the look on her face this morning was quite funny. She looked at me for almost five seconds before figuring out that Elliot was missing. It was hysterical to see her crawling on hands and knees, looking to see if he fell off and landed under a chair or the sofa. Her butt was so high in the air, and it wiggled in the funniest way as she inched forward. We couldn't look at each other for fear of laughing out loud.

Once she gave up on trying to finding El, she made a breakfast of eggs and bacon. The bacon smelled so, so good. Ron awoke to the smells, and they ate in the kitchenette overlooking the garden in the backyard. A little bunny rabbit made an appearance, and Katie tossed a carrot out the back door in his direction.

Once the breakfast dishes were put in the dishwasher, the kitchen really got busy. Katie cleaned a turkey and wrapped it in foil, then placed it in the oven. She retrieved several bowls and plates from the cabinets, then made a label for each food item she was going to make. Each plate or bowl got tagged. From the looks of the labels, a feast was going down tonight.

Ron went outside for a while, then came back in and turned on the television. He was watching another one of those football games. In a football game, one person throws or hands another person a ball. Then half the people on the playing field try to kill the man with the ball, and half of the people try to stop the first team from killing their man. A lot of other stuff goes on, but that is the main idea.

Humans. Go figure.

It was a relaxing day filled with happiness. I grasped that all we do and strive for is happiness. I was glad I already had everything I needed to feel that way. Randy was able to play at night, Elliot was where he was meant to be, and Santa Steve had gotten to meet *the man.* Before he left, Saint Nick promised to say hello each year, even if we were in the closet and not in the front room. That made Santa Steve extremely happy.

I was glad Hula was so good at using her imagination. In a way, she did get to travel, but I couldn't help but search for possibilities to make world travel a reality for her.

Over dinner, Katie and Ron were talking about last nights' party and their goals for the New Year. They played a game during which Katie asked Ron his biggest most audacious goal for the coming year. Ron talked about expanding his computer company and ways to improve customer service.

When it was Katie's turn, she proved that she knew how to dream big. She decided that our story, the story about "The Most Beautiful Ugly Sweater in the World" needed to be told. She planned to write a novel and get it published before next Christmas.

She articulated her thoughts of creating a great marketing plan and being featured on television shows. She spoke of all the cities in which she would do book signings and interviews. It was called a book tour. And she told Ron she would wear me all the time.

Of course, this would mean Hula could travel to many different places as we went on this book tour, generating publicity for her new book. I was elated.

What a perfect end to a perfect day! Hula had pretended her way into having all her dreams come true for real. All those that I love got exactly what they wanted, and I would have a sister visiting me soon while Katlin and Miya decorated her together. I wondered what sort of family my sister would get, or if they would use the exact same decorations Katie attached to me.

Later that night when I was in the closet and Ron and Katie were getting ready for bed, I heard this soft gentle voice, almost a whisper.

"You have done well my precious one. I am proud of you."

Much to my surprise, I looked and saw it was my angel … the one on top of my tree. She was glowing brightly and had a soft, radiant luminosity that was comforting.

I stared in stunned silence, and it was a full minute before I collected myself enough to speak. "We thought you were a non-thinker. You can talk? Why haven't you said anything until now?" I asked.

"I am not just any angel; I am your guardian angel," the winged beauty responded. "Throughout the year I silently watch over you. When you need my help, I will whisper in your ear. My voice is so soft you won't hear it, but my words will join with your heart, and you will know which direction is best for you.

My name is Seraphina, and once a year, on Christmas night, you will be able to hear me."

We spoke for hours, everyone asking different questions of my new friend and personal angel. Her words of wisdom, ages of knowledge, and timeless truths had us captivated. Even as I drifted off to sleep, her words echoed in my mind, and I felt a new calling that was magnetic even in my slumber. I dreamt that I wrote the Scrolls of Seraphina, and each year I would write a new scroll sharing her timeless truths. Young people would read her book and confidently go out into life, doing great things. It was a great dream, and I was reluctant to wake up this morning.

Thursday, December 26
Dear Diary,

I woke up thinking that I was going to make the rest of my life, the best of my life. I feel safe and secure knowing my angel Seraphina will always be silently watching me. One of the things she told me last night is that everyone has a guardian angel, even if they cannot see theirs. I was glad everyone got to have one.

I have learned so much over the last month, diary.

I have learned the importance of friends, staying positive, having faith in the universe and so much more.

I hope my writing has inspired you, and I promise to write more as we travel the world sharing our lessons with everyone.

Thank you, diary, for being my faithful friend, as well. I really appreciate having you here to listen to me anytime I need you. Merry Christmas ... and remember, you have the power to make it the best New Year ever!

I'm beautiful. You're beautiful. We're all beautiful!
~ Sophie the Sweater

Acknowledgements

When you complete a major undertaking such as writing a book, it comes as no surprise that there are many people to thank. I want to start with my family, as they have a lot to do with who I am and all I accomplish. They are my loving husband, John; my adoring mom Pat Eubank; my wonderful son Leif Johnsen and amazing daughter-in-law Elissa; and my grandson Elliot.

While I do not see the rest of my family as often, my brothers, sisters, aunts, uncles, nephews, nieces and other various relatives are all etched in my heart. I love you dearly Marci, Jess, Chloe, Tim, Irina, Tatiana, Tom, Cornelia, Larry, Mary Ann, Richard, Deborah, Ricky, Ann, Robby, Jake, Austin, Leila, Tonya, Aunt Kay, Uncle Leo, Aunt Sue, Mark, Terry, Kevin, Kurt, Mike, Ann, Tom, Stacy, Debbie, Paul and Carrie, Ronnie and Melissa..

My great love and admiration goes out to Leigh LeCreux, without whom the completion of this book may never have come to fruition. You are priceless in so many ways, for so many reasons.

My daughter/sister/best friend Nikole Schlittenhardt was there every step of the way, and I am always grateful for her love and support. Love you Nik.

To John Weis, my wonderful editor, thank you for making me look good. I greatly appreciate you!

And Christy Cooper Blanc, my first editor!

To Sabrina Fajardo, thank you for the beautiful artwork that graces the cover of this book.

Thank you, Ron Bates, for always reminding us that it starts at the shoulder.

My undying gratitude goes out to Wendy Baron, who is my partner in manifesting great magic in this world.

To Laura Baron, thank you for being a lifelong role model and a woman I love and respect greatly.

Big respect and admiration goes out to Lois Margolin, who has supported me in all I do while setting a great example for anyone who knows her.

For those no longer with us who have shaped my life and are still watching over me, you have my love. Steve Baron, Jesse Lee Eubank, Joe Scheefers, Celeste McKinney, Helen Quinlivan, Thomas Quinlivan, Eleanor Snyder, and Naomi Murph.

Thank you to those I rarely see, yet who seem to rarely leave me: Kevin Anthony Flores, Peggy Powell … and many others.

But this book is for you, my reader. With deepest gratitude, I give you my most sincere thanks for taking your time to delight in the tale the universe has entrusted me with sharing … joining me on this journey through my imagination. It is a sacred space that we have shared.

Cassi Eubank is dubbed "The Results Coach" because she knows how to take a person's vision, help them get clarity, and show them how to storyboard their success.

Life has taught her that retaining a childlike quality of wonder keeps her in touch with her creative side. This allows her to first see, and then manifest, the things she loves in her life.

Cassi produced and hosted a television show on the FOX network for nearly five years. *Home Grown Music* featured local and national acts on her show including Matchbox Twenty, Collective Soul, Kansas, Kid Rock, and more. In addition, she has also hosted two radio shows, and is the author of two other books. *Do You Know Elvis* was a best seller at the Elvis Days Celebration, moving almost 1,000 copies in one weekend.

Now, she turns her attention to the creative world of fiction, to deliver the powerful life lessons she shares with her clients with the high risk youth she nurtures. Her passion for helping teens overcome the life challenges they encounter prompted her to create a companion guide, which will enable people to take the lessons that Sophie has learned and apply it to their own lives.

Cassi is happily married to John Scheefers. The couple lives in Boca Raton, Florida with their German Shepherd Rocky. She is blessed with a wonderful son, Leif Johnsen; daughter-in-law Elissa; and grandchild, Elliot Johnsen. The visionary also loves travel, singing, gardening, beaches and all that life has to offer.

For more information about Cassi Eubank or to bring Cassi to your next event please email Cassi@CassiEubank.com or visit www.CassiEubank.com.

Heroes and Champions

Although one person may author a book, it takes a wonderful support group to see a project through. I want to express my very deep appreciation to my heroes and champions. These are the people who were able to see my vision with me and gave me the love, encouragement and full support to bring this dream to life. I will never forget these people and now that they are in these pages, please let their names be a reminder of the importance of friends and family in your life as well.

Pat Eubank
Kay Quinlivan
Shirley Groser
Judy Rubin
Shirah Penn
Carrol Wilkinson
Sherrie Glusky Gottesman
David Pollock
Rovy Pollock
Carolyn Reigle Lawrence
Kay Reigle Snelling
Wendy Umble
Orit Murad Rehany
Jay Elias
Judy Lee Thurber
Jenny Bedell
Kelly Salazar
Donna Knox
Valerie Brunnberg
Jason Whitley
Jennifer Bridgers

My Heroes and Champions

Joy Agness
Lois Margolin
Stacy Aberle
Lisa Prosen
Alicia Couri
Jason Montgomery
Miya Montgomery
Molly Schmidt
Kim Shivler
Sherri Frost
Adele Alexandre
Irma Parone
The Wyatt family
Suzanne Kovi
Kathy Gallagher
Vivien Balcker
Dr. Paula Liebeskind
Fay Wilmont
Sharon Maupin
Joyce Belanger

Angels Are Never Forgotten

There are those who are in our lives for too short a time. They touch our hearts and then return to spirit to guide us the rest of the way. The love they have given us keeps us strong and if we listen closely we can hear their voices. We may not be able to touch them in the physical sense any longer, but they will always touch us with their memory and the gifts they have left us with. Here is to angels and those who have enriched our lives and those of everyone on the planet, just by have lived.

Jesse Lee Eubank
Stephen Baron
Joe Scheefers
Helen Quinlivan
Thomas Quinlivan
Eleanor Snyder
Naomi Parish
Celeste McKinney
William Dovgala
Paul Scheefers
Maxine Scheefers
Christina Durham
Lizzy Groser
Ric Valdes
Bette Reynolds
Gina Carlone Valenti

www.DiaryOfAnUglySweater.com

Made in the USA
Charleston, SC
09 May 2015